BLUE FIRE

BLUE FIRE

RED RAIN #5

RACHEL NEWHOUSE

rachelnewhouse.com

To Dylan—
You're the bee's knees

JUNE 2076

1

The last person I wanted to see was my mother.

She wasn't my biological mother, of course; that woman had been dead for years. No, Mrs. Nolan was my mother in name only, and not by choice. I hadn't wanted to be adopted. I hadn't wanted to change my name and use the file Thames—Mr. Nolan—had forged for me.

But I'd had no choice. I'd had no choice, because Thames had forced me to record videos taking responsibility for the destruction of the factory on Rott. He'd sacrificed me as a scapegoat so that the United wouldn't know he'd been manufacturing a world-ending superweapon. He'd let me take the blame and turned my whole family into public enemies.

That's why I recorded a video and revealed his identity to the government. That's why he killed himself. That's why I altered my fingerprints, assumed the identity he'd created for me, and ran.

I never wanted to see Mrs. Nolan again, but now she stood at the end of the hall, between me and the only exit. Why was she here? She had no reason to be here. We were in an office building on the fringes of downtown Boston that had been converted into a base for the underground. It was supposed to be a safe place, or at least that's what my old classmate Stanyard had said when he'd brought me here.

Now I was beginning to wonder if I'd walked right into another prison.

I scrambled up from the floor and braced myself, feet apart. Mrs. Nolan didn't move. She studied me, not saying anything for a cold minute. She looked exactly the same as she had the last time we'd met. Her hair had been flat-ironed into submission, and her lips were a perfect shade of pink.

Only this time, she wasn't smiling.

"Andromeda," she said, using my adopted name. There was no emotion attached to it.

I clenched my fists. "What do you want?"

She took me in once, twice; I swore I saw her grimace in displeasure. "We need to talk."

"No, no—you need to leave me alone." I'd spent the last several weeks fighting to get away from the Nolans; I wasn't going back.

"Philadelphia," my older brother Ephesus called to me from where he sat on the floor.

I glanced back at him. He met my eyes and spoke slowly. "It's okay. She's with me."

The hallway flashed out of focus as the universe shattered around him.

No. Don't do this to me.

"She's *with* you?"

He nodded.

My heart throbbed in my ears. I glanced at the others in the room, willing them to discredit the story.

Jayde, the soldier who was supposed to be in charge of this place, just shrugged.

I turned to Stanyard. His dark eyes were guarded as he said, "She helped us find you."

I sucked in a breath but didn't get any air. "You led her right to me."

You betrayed me. Again.

"Phil, it's okay," Ephesus repeated. "I promise you can trust her."

His words pierced my chest like a needle. "Trust her? You have no idea what she's done!"

"What did I do, Andromeda?"

I spun around. Mrs. Nolan crossed her arms, expression calm and pale. "What did I do to you?"

I gaped at her as the rejection filled my lungs like water. "What did you do to me? Do you have *any* idea how much hell your husband put me through?"

"Phil!" Ephesus exclaimed.

"Wow, someone's upset," Jayde remarked.

"They kidnapped me! They drugged me and took me to another *planet*," I screamed, as if I had to justify it. Why did I have to justify my feelings? Why didn't anyone understand?

Why doesn't anyone care?

Mrs. Nolan was unmoved. "Sweetheart, you know it was for your own good."

The butter—the sugary compromise that I knew all too well—slipped back into her voice, and my stomach hurled. "My own good? You used me as blackmail, and now the government wants to kill me. It's your fault I had to change my name. It's your fault Philadelphia's gone."

You planned this. You planned it this way all along, and you know it.

She shook her head. "And you *would* be dead if it weren't for that file my husband forged for you. We only did it to protect you."

"Protect me?" I screeched, but my voice broke at the end. My throat burned, and every breath made my bruised rib hurt. It didn't matter anyway—no one was listening to me.

Ephesus grabbed my hand and tried to drag me back down to the ground beside him. "Phil, please, I promise I can explain everything."

I wrenched my hand from his grasp. "No, you can't." *There's nothing you can say that will fix this.*

The realization hit me like a fresh kick to the ribs. There was a time when my big brother could have fixed anything. Now he sounded just like one of them.

I started to cry.

Stanyard put his hands up. "Hey, it's okay. You need to sit down, breathe."

He took a step towards me. I backed away—right into the wall. My pulse shot to my throat.

I don't trust you. I don't trust any of you.

"He's right." Ephesus pushed himself to his feet with his good arm, and suddenly the hallway seemed a lot narrower. "Let's all step back and regroup."

He touched my shoulder, and I threw him off. "Don't touch me!"

Jayde reacted. "All right, that's enough." He reached forward to grab me, one muscular hand sliding reflexively towards his holstered gun.

I ran.

I turned and sprinted down the hall. Someone shouted my name, but I wasn't sure who. I heard heavy footsteps behind me and willed myself to be faster.

At least Mrs. Nolan had the decency to get out of the way.

I'd never make it on the elevator. I turned the corner and followed the exit signs to the nearest stairwell. I threw the door open and slid down the stairs, taking them three at a time. I had to get out of sight before they figured out which floor I was on. The building was huge; surely there was some place to hide.

I descended until I reached the basement. I slid around the door and shoved it shut behind me, pausing to listen. Shouts echoed from further up the stairwell, but they were several floors away.

The corridor was dark except for a lone security light. I stumbled around until I found an alcove out of sight of the stairwell and collapsed on the ground.

The adrenaline broke, and in its place rolled waves of pain. My injured side was screaming. It wasn't the first time I'd been kicked in the ribs, but the pain was infinitely worse than I remembered. Ambrose's kicks had been fat and clumsy. Carnegie wasn't strong, but he was cruel. He had known exactly where to kick to make me bruise.

I braced myself against the wall and struggled not to vomit. I was shaking and sweating and saw flashing colors, even though the hall was dark.

Oh God, help.

What was I going to do? I was stranded on Earth with a dozen enemies. The government was hunting for me; the underground had compromised my position and almost gotten me killed; and my own brother was partnering with the one woman who could reveal my identity and condemn me to death.

Meanwhile, my dad, the person I had come back to Earth to save, was cryogenically frozen, and the one man who could probably fix everything was on another planet.

You should have stayed on Mars, sweetheart.

"Philadelphia."

I screamed. Ephesus stood over me. He looked terrifying backlit by the weak security lighting, with his shaved head and bandaged nose and everything that was strange and unfamiliar.

I hid my face. "Leave me alone!"

He knelt beside me. "What's wrong? You're white. Are you hurt?"

He reached towards me. I jerked back and winced. "Please don't touch me," I whimpered. It was a plea this time, not a command. *Everything hurts so bad.*

"Phil, please, you need to see a doctor. Let Mrs. Nolan look at you."

"No!" She was the last person I wanted to touch me.

He sighed. He sounded annoyed, which just made me want to cry. "Phil, I promise she won't hurt you."

You don't know that. I tucked myself further into the corner. "You don't understand."

"You're right—I don't."

I stopped and looked up at him.

He searched my face. "I have no idea what you've been through—because I wasn't there."

The statement held no accusation, only heartbreak. He sat cross-legged on the floor next to me. "I have no idea what happened between you and Thames. Cynthia—Mrs. Nolan—told me what she knows, and I saw your videos, but I know that's only half the story. I know you've been through a nightmare, and I wasn't there to help you."

His voice cracked. "We've barely seen each other these past two years, and that kills me. Honestly, Phil, when you came around the corner back there," he gestured at the floors above us, "I didn't even recognize you."

I grimaced, but I wasn't surprised. In the process of becoming Andromeda, I'd chopped my long, dark hair and bleached it nearly white. I wore blue contacts and had three piercings in my ears; not to mention, my new aesthetic of ripped jeans and angsty t-shirts was a far cry from the industrial skirt and jacket I used to wear. I didn't look anything like the girl he'd left behind.

You aren't the girl he left behind. That girl is dead.

Ephesus's eyes glistened in the dark. "I don't even know you anymore, and it's my fault. I feel like I failed you. You had to fight for your life, and you had to do it alone."

But you weren't alone, the Holy Spirit reminded me. Nic had been there for me—or at least he had been until I'd run away to Earth because I thought I could fix everything.

A fresh sob ripped out of me.

"Oh Philli." Ephesus gently took my hand. "I know I wasn't there for you, but I'm here now. You don't have to do this by yourself. We'll get through this together. Just please, let me—let us—help you."

I flinched. That was the exact same thing Thames had said to me.

Let me help you.

I took a deep breath and tried to steady my thoughts. I didn't trust Mrs. Nolan. I had no idea what she expected to gain by partnering with Ephesus, but it couldn't be good. I also didn't trust Jayde or the underground; they'd already lied to me more than once. And Stanyard—he'd saved my life today, but only after he put it in danger. I still didn't know where he stood.

But even if I couldn't count them as friends, I knew I could trust Ephesus. He'd made mistakes, but he was still my brother. And that was something even a name change couldn't take from me.

I opened my mouth to respond, but approaching footsteps interrupted me. Stanyard rounded the corner.

"I'm sorry," he panted with a nervous glance at me, "but they've brought your dad in."

2

He's not dead, he's not dead, he's not dead.

I chanted it over and over to make myself believe it. He certainly looked dead. His petrified face screamed out from beneath the glass, and the shadow of his twisted body was faintly visible through the solid block of green-blue cryoprotectant. To make matters worse, the flickering displays and throbbing controls made the whole apparatus look like it was glowing. Dad's terrified features appeared rotten and taut in the green light, like he'd fallen into a vat of acid and burned alive.

I stumbled and braced myself against the doorframe. *He's not dead, he's not dead. Dad's not dead.*

They'd dragged Dad's preservation tube up to a lab on the fifth floor of the base. The microscopes and racks of bottles had been swept aside to make room for the bulky machine. The coffin-sized tube was propped up at an angle and connected to a computer terminal by a net of wires. Mrs. Nolan stood at the screen, tampering with the monitor.

"Get away from him!" I screeched.

She glanced over her shoulder. "What this man needs is a doctor, and I'm the only one you have right now."

I opened my mouth, but Ephesus squeezed my arm. "Phil, please, let me handle this."

He walked over to Mrs. Nolan and whispered something. I didn't like the way he approached her. He stood close, too close, their shoulders nearly brushing, and he spoke to her like they'd been friends for years. He really did trust her.

Do you not have any idea who she is?

A lanky teenager I didn't recognize was wiring the machine into the wall. He finished and straightened with a grunt. "You'd better come up with a good excuse for this power drain, or you can expect an audit in the morning," he declared to no one in particular, his words thickened by a Russian accent. He couldn't have been more than thirteen or fourteen, and puberty had not yet altered his voice. The preteen squeak undermined the gruffness of his accent, and the effect was like salt on a wound.

He wiped his greasy hands on his jeans and turned to face me. He sized me up with eyes the color of faded denim. "Blue Fire," he acknowledged with a nod.

I stiffened. "Blue Fire" was the callsign the underground had invented for me on the radio, and I had no love for it. I eyed the young man. "Who are you?"

"Lev," he replied. "But you know me as Watts." He ran a hand through his buzzed blond hair and waited for a reaction.

My whole face tightened in disgust. Watts had been one of the many voices on the radio, one of the members of the underground who had stalked me and led me right into the path of a bullet.

Yet another person I can't trust.

Jayde inadvertently diffused the room. "I'll take care of the power drain. Good work, man," he said, and gave Lev a hefty pat on the back. Lev nodded and saw himself out, giving me one last look as he passed.

I found the courage to step into the room. Stanyard, who had been hovering behind me in the hall, followed at a safe distance.

Mrs. Nolan went back to maneuvering the controls. Ephesus leaned over the tube and looked in.

I approached his side. He stood there, staring, for minutes that felt like hours, not making a sound. I willed him—or me—to say something. Scream, accuse, demand, apologize, anything. But I couldn't come up with the words.

Ephesus, I'm so sorry.

Finally, his lips moved, but no sound came out. It took me a minute to realize he was praying.

He took a deep breath and turned to Jayde. "We need a revival tech. Do you know anyone?"

Jayde stalled by chewing on his lip. "There's someone I can call. But his track record is not... great."

I grabbed Dad's tube with a protective hand, then regretted it when the frost bit my fingertips. "No! Dad only has one chance. We can't risk it."

Ephesus nodded. He wiped a hand across his pallid forehead. "She's right. He's better off frozen than poorly revived."

Mrs. Nolan stabbed at the screen. "No, he's not."

I turned to her. She glared at me with eyes colder than the machine beneath my hand. "The longer he's frozen, the more therapy he'll need. More of his skin will have to be regenerated, and he'll lose most of his organs. He'll need additional transplants—and the longer he's under, the more his likelihood of surviving those procedures drops."

Her words sent despair rippling through my nerves, but I forced a straight face. "We're doing it right—with a technician I trust."

If she heard the insult, she didn't react. Ephesus glanced between us before turning to Jayde.

"I'll make some calls," he grunted, then left.

Stanyard moved aside to let him pass, then looked at me. "Can I get you some water, Phil?"

"I'm fine," I said without pausing to ascertain if that was true.

He tried again. "Have you eaten? You're still pale. You need to rest."

"He's right." Ephesus laid his hand gently on my shoulder. "You should lie down."

"I'm not leaving Dad," I declared with all the authority I could muster, but my voice came out paper-thin.

Ephesus shook his head. "There's nothing you can do for him right now."

"But I—"

"He's right," Mrs. Nolan inserted. "None of us can do anything until the machine stabilizes. It has to recalibrate after it's been unplugged for transport. I can't even get into the diagnostics until it finishes its cycle." She swiped fruitlessly at the screen.

Ephesus tried to steer me out of the room. "Come on, let's find you someplace to sleep."

"No!" I screamed, then paused to figure out why that thought filled me with such dread. I grabbed Ephesus's arm. "Don't leave me alone—please."

He searched my face, his own expression pinched. "Okay."

Stanyard excused himself. Ephesus took my hand and led me out of the lab. I followed him down a floor to a lounge stuffed with couches and recliners. Ephesus turned off the lights and propped the door open so that the room was lit only by the gentle glow from the security lamps in the hallway. He rooted around in a cabinet until he found a blanket, then gestured at the biggest couch. I sat down, and he settled in next to me.

He draped the blanket over my knees and put his good arm around my shoulder. I collapsed against him, just like I'd always done with Dad.

It wasn't the same.

He didn't say anything for a long moment. "You need to rest."

"I don't want to sleep."

"Okay." He didn't ask for an explanation. "You don't have to." He shifted so he was settled back in the cushions. I tried to copy him, but I felt stiff and rigid, no matter how much I willed my nerves to relax.

Ephesus noticed. "Try talking to me. Tell me everything that happened."

I didn't want to recap the nightmare again, but Ephesus needed to know. I wanted him to know.

He rubbed my shoulder. "Start from the beginning."

*

I was drowning.

I was submerged in a sea of green-blue. I fought and twisted, but I couldn't see any source of light, any sand on the floor, any indication of which way was up. I gasped but didn't swallow anything—no air, no water. No sound left my lips, and I panicked.

Somebody help me!

The water was thick and slimy. Each stroke was exhausting, and the more I pushed, the more the water pushed back. *Is the water getting harder?*

"Philadelphia?"

I heard my name and a distant knocking, but I couldn't tell which direction it came from. I screamed fruitlessly.

You have to help me!

I stretched my hand forward—and rammed my knuckles into something solid. The sea of green had become cold, hard, and slick.

Ice.

I swung my other arm and slammed my elbow into more ice. I tried to kick my legs, but I couldn't move them at all. The water seized around me in a solid block of ice. I couldn't move my arms, or my head, or my lungs. I couldn't breathe, and it was getting colder.

You're freezing. You're going to die—

"Phil!"

A warm hand touched my shoulder, and the nightmare shattered.

I jerked upright, reality washing over me like a bucket of water. There was someone close—too close—and I didn't recognize the room, and my heart was still pounding, and I—

"Whoa, hey, it's okay, you're okay."

I focused on the face. It was Stanyard. He stood over me, which did nothing to ease the panic. I scooted away from him. "What are you doing here?"

He put his hands up. "I'm sorry, I tried to wake you by knocking on the door, but you were out."

I took another stock of the room and finally remembered where I was. I was alone on the couch, the blanket tucked around me. Daylight illuminated the hallway outside. "Where's Ephesus?"

"I can't find him—that's why I came to get you."

I heard the tremor in his voice and looked up. "What's wrong?"

His eyes took a full lap of the room before they met mine. "There's a problem."

3

I threw the blanket aside and stood up, ignoring the flash of pain in my ribs. Stanyard took the cue and led the way.

I followed him back to the lab. They'd hooked Dad's tube to half a dozen additional monitors; the tiny room was now crammed with machines. Their motors hummed at an unnatural pitch and their displays flickered with unstable readouts—an irritable pulsing that perfectly matched the adrenaline that was still draining from my system.

"What is it?" I asked, fighting to keep my voice calm, even though my mind leapt to a dozen apocalyptic conclusions.

Stanyard pointed at the main control panel. "The machine is password-protected. We can't thaw it without the code." He dropped his arm. "And I'm guessing that code was Carnegie's."

Who is very, extremely, dead.

My heart thudded against my ribcage, all the panic and distress and grief battering to get out. I took a quick breath—too quick, the sound coming out like a sharp gasp. Stanyard flinched.

I took another breath, slower this time. "Can you hack the password?"

"I can try running a decryption program. I just wanted to ask you first."

I answered him almost before he finished the sentence. "Yes, please."

He nodded. "It will take a while for the program to run, depending on how long and complicated his password is. I'll come get you when I have something to report. You should go back to bed—"

"I'll wait."

He studied me for a beat. "Okay. I'll go get my computer."

He returned ten minutes later with a backpack overflowing with wires and gadgetry. I watched from a safe distance as he pried a panel off the control monitor, exposing an access port. He fished through his bag until he found the right adaptor and plugged it in. Then, with a swift and confident hand, he started weaving a Medusa's head of wires. He plugged different cords and adaptors together—feeding some through flashing devices he procured from his bag—before finally connecting a cable to his laptop.

"I'm surprised all of this isn't wireless," I commented in fascination.

"You don't want a machine like this to be wireless." He turned his laptop on. "If it was, anyone on the internet could hack into it."

I swallowed. I definitely didn't want a stranger halfway across the planet to have access to Dad's tube.

Stanyard wheeled a desk chair up to the control panel, propped his laptop on his knees, and started typing. I figured he didn't want me staring over his shoulder the entire time, so I dragged another chair to the other side of the machine and sat down next to Dad.

I didn't look at him; I didn't need his terrified face etched in my nightmares any more than it already was. Instead, I traced my fingernail through the frost on the glass and prayed silently. The only sound in the lab was the irregular clack of Stanyard's keyboard.

I glanced over the machine at him. He was angled away from me, his uncombed dark hair fringed in a blue glow from his laptop screen. I thanked God that Stanyard was willing to help, even as I wondered if he would be able to do it. Stanyard had been hacking for as long as I'd known him—he'd gone to detention for messing with the school's computers more times than I could count—but there was a big difference between altering someone's algebra grades and breaking into a secured cryogenics tube.

But then again, he'd accomplished some intense hacking for me while I was on Mars. Altering the door lock database couldn't have been easy—unless that was Jayde's handiwork.

With a flush of frustration, I realized I still had no idea how much of "Aurelius"—the mysterious online user who had helped me escape from Thames—was Jayde and how much was Stanyard. For all I knew, Jayde had done the heavy lifting.

Either way, I deserved to know.

"Hey."

"Yeah?" he responded without looking up.

"While I was on Mars…"

He stopped typing.

"How much of that was you talking?"

"Jayde dictated a little." There was an audible beat. "The rest was me."

I drew circles in the fog on the glass, replaying all of the messages I had received from Aurelius over in my mind.

I'D RATHER NOT WATCH THAMES KILL YOU ON LIVESTREAM IF IT CAN BE AVOIDED

"Did you do all that hacking yourself?"

He scrolled on his laptop, but I could tell he wasn't really working. "It was a team effort. Jayde had access to the programs, but I did a lot of the legwork."

DID YOU SLEEP AT ALL?

DID YOU?

YEAH ACTUALLY

GOOD

Suddenly his late-night efforts and quick responses took on a new meaning, and I wondered why I hadn't seen it before.

I NEVER GOT A CHANCE TO SAY THANK YOU

DON'T

But then again, why would I think it was him? He was the last person I expected to help. All he'd ever done was prove that he didn't care about me, and he'd abandoned me time and again when I needed him most.

I never once imagined he'd come back to get me.

IT'S THE LEAST I CAN DO

An unease gripped my chest. "Did you mean what you said?"
"Which part?" he responded, too quickly.
"Everything," I said firmly.

I'M SORRY PHIL. I REALLY AM

He was silent. I stared at the back of his head—waiting, as always, for him to turn around.
Finally, he did. "Everything I said was the truth."
"Except the part about you being Jayde."
His eyes drifted again. "I never actually said I was…"
I sighed. "Why didn't you just tell me?"
"I didn't…" He stopped and recalculated, as if he wisely deduced that I wouldn't buy any more excuses.
He slammed his laptop shut. "I was scared. Okay? I was afraid that if I told you it was me, you'd block me—or give me the look you're giving me now."
I tried to figure out what expression was reading on my face, but I had no idea how I felt. I had no idea how I felt about any of this.

"All I wanted was the truth," I squeaked, and suddenly started to cry, hard.

"Phil…" I heard the desk chair roll across the floor and felt him in front of me. His fingers brushed my shoulder.

"Don't touch me!" I screeched, and slapped him away. The sharp sound of flesh on flesh broke through the throbbing in my ears, and I realized what I'd done. Stanyard had saved me from Carnegie, and now he was trying to save my dad, and all I'd done was scream at him.

What is wrong with you?

"I'm sorry, I'm sorry, I'm sorry," I gushed, trying to stuff the emotions back where they came from. But the more I tried to silence the anger and the fear, the more it roared. I felt scared and unsafe and exposed, and all I could do was sob and wish the tears would break something down inside of me.

They didn't.

It was several minutes before Stanyard spoke again. "Philadelphia."

He waited until I stopped crying. I swallowed the last sob and wiped my eyes, then stared at my hands in my lap.

He knelt to get in my line of sight. "Philadelphia, I'm sorry. I'm sorry I lied to you. I'm sorry I left you behind. I almost got you killed, and I've never regretted anything more in my life."

I believed him, but it didn't make me feel any better—or make me feel anything at all.

He didn't wait for a response. "I'm sorry for everything." And then, without missing a beat, he added: "Will you forgive me?"

Time stopped, and I gaped at him. No one had ever asked me to forgive them. Ephesus hadn't. Dad hadn't. Nic certainly hadn't, but I wasn't going to wait up for that one. Sure, I knew all of them were sorry by their actions—just like I knew Stanyard was sorry by his—but none of them had never *asked.*

Of course, it was a rhetorical question, wasn't it? Obviously, I had to forgive him. The Bible left no room for interpretation on that matter.

I opened my mouth to give the reflexive response, but he put his hand up. "No," he said, very firmly. "I don't want you to say it just because we're Christians and that's what we're supposed to say."

I frowned at him. "How do you want me to say it, then?"

He didn't hesitate. "I want you to say it like you said it to your dad."

I instinctively glanced at the block of ice beside me. I pictured the recording studio, with the camera whirring and my eyes blurring and the rage burning inside of me—and through it all a strong, confident feeling that I was doing the right thing, even if it broke me down to the core of my soul.

I forgive you.

I swallowed. "I don't... I don't know if I trust you like that." *Yet*, I should have added, but didn't.

He wasn't offended by the omission. "You weren't sure if you trusted your dad, either."

I still didn't—at least not in the same way I used to. There was still a lot I didn't understand, a lot we needed to work through. But as I stared at his body, mercilessly enshrined in glass, I knew without a doubt that my hurt and my pain wouldn't come between us, no matter how long it took to heal.

Because I'd forgiven him.

"I know I need to earn your trust back." Stanyard's whisper caused me to look back at him. "That could take months, years—I don't care."

"Then what do you want from me?" *What are you expecting?*

His dark eyes were raw and unfiltered as he declared, "I want you to give me a chance."

I searched his face.

"I know it will take time. But if you're going to say you forgive me, I need you to mean it. I need to know that you're wiping that from my account and letting it go. I need to know that when I try, you're not going to remind me of all my past sins—that every time I hold out my hand, you're not thinking of the time I left you behind."

He glanced down at his own hands then, and the images flashed before my eyes unbidden.

"I... don't know if I can do that," I stuttered. "Because right now, that's all I see."

"I know," he whispered, voice beyond broken.

I struggled to piece my feelings together. "I know you tried to make it up to me on Mars, but our whole relationship was based on a lie. And now every time I look at you, I have to ask myself if you're still lying."

He didn't defend himself, but he lifted his face to meet mine.

I quickly looked away. "And what am I supposed to do? Tell you I never want to see you again? I need you to hack Dad's tube. I need you, and I hate that I need you, but I don't have a choice. I *have* to forgive you."

There, at least I said it.

His tone was firm and unflinching as he responded. "I'll do everything I can to save your dad whether you forgive me or not. This isn't conditional. But if you're going to forgive me, I need you to mean it. I need you to give me the opportunity to earn your trust."

The silence was pregnant, so I knew I had to look at him. "And what if I don't?"

Rejection flooded his eyes. My conscience writhed, but I didn't back down. I had to know. I had to know if I really had a choice.

"Then I guess I'll have to live with that," he whispered. "But at least I asked."

The pain in his voice stabbed me, but at the same time, I felt powerful, like he'd handed me a gun with the safety off. For the first time in years, I had a choice. It was my decision, and the only person I had to answer to was God.

And there was always a choice with God.

Stanyard pinched his eyes shut. When he looked at me again, his expression was deep and clear. "I'm giving you my weapons, Phil. If you're going to shoot me, do it. But don't say 'I forgive you' if you don't mean it. I can't live that way." He took in a sharp breath and let it out. "Not with you."

Something caught in the back of my throat, but for once, I didn't fear the feeling.

"Philadelphia," Stanyard said again, his tone resetting the room. "Will you forgive me?"

I inhaled and sat up straight. "Yes, I will."

He didn't smile, but I saw the life creep back into his eyes. "Thank you."

He stood up before I could think of anything else to say. "It's going to take me a little while to get my decryption program set up. I need to reconfigure it to work with this OS."

I took the hint this time. "I should go find Ephesus. Text me when you make progress." I stood up and walked to the door.

He returned to his chair and started clacking on his laptop again. I stopped in the doorway and watched him work for a fraction of a second.

"Hey."

He paused and glanced up.

"Will you let me say 'thank you' now?"

Something close to a smile stretched his lips. "You're welcome, Phil."

I smiled back, then left, shutting the door behind me.

4

Ephesus found me as soon as I walked out of the lab. He came jogging down the hall, calling my name.

"There you are! What's wrong? I had a dozen missed calls from Stanyard, and then you were gone…"

I swallowed and forced the truth out before I could choke on it. "Dad's tube is password-protected."

He stopped in front of me and ran through the requisite cycle of emotions, finally settling on bitterness. "Carnegie."

I nodded, and the motion shook more tears loose. "Ephesus, I'm so sorry—"

"Phil, stop, please." He touched my shoulder and glanced through the window into the lab. "Is Stanyard trying to hack it?"

I nodded again and rubbed my eyes. "He's configuring his password programs to work with the system."

"Then we should let him work." Ephesus steered me down the hall. "Come get breakfast."

I glanced up at him as we walked into the elevator. I thought about asking him where he'd been, but I answered my own question when I saw his buzzed hair was glistening wet.

For the first time, I took a moment to acknowledge the changes in his appearance. I missed his fluffy hair already, and I wondered how mutilated his nose was under the bandage.

He caught me staring and reached up to touch it. "I promise it's not bad. They just splinted it to keep it from getting bent out of shape while it healed."

I stepped onto the elevator after him. "And your arm? Can't they just regenerate the bone?"

"Sure, but you have to go to a special facility for that." He adjusted the strap of his gaudy orange sling as we descended a few floors. "Thames was trying to keep this whole thing off the radar, so he couldn't risk checking me into a 'real' hospital. So it's the old-fashioned cast and sling for me."

The elevator door dinged and opened, and we stepped out into the hall. I heard chattering voices and clattering dishes from up ahead.

"I promise I'm fine. Cynthia—Mrs. Nolan says she'll probably take the splint off my nose this week." He looked down at me with that generous, trustworthy smile that used to solve all my problems—but now I could barely feel the warmth.

I weakly returned the gesture, just so he wouldn't worry.

We rounded the corner into a small cafeteria. A few people I didn't recognize littered the tables. Mrs. Nolan and Jayde stood around the prep counter, talking. They both stopped and looked up at me.

"Blue Fire!" Jayde boomed, tipping his coffee mug towards me.

I flinched. "Don't call me that."

Jayde opened his mouth, but Ephesus came to my defense. "Her name is Philadelphia."

"It's actually Andromeda," Mrs. Nolan returned.

The dissonant names ricocheted around in my head, making the world spin as a dozen conflicting realities collided like black holes. I wanted to slap my hands over my ears and shut them all out.

You have no idea who I am.

Jayde must have read my expression, because his face softened. "You're right, I'm sorry—you haven't even had coffee yet." He took the carafe off the warmer. "How do you take it?"

I took in a full breath and let it out, expelling all the fluttering thoughts with it. "Black, please."

Jayde blinked. "Whoa, hardcore."

Ephesus blanched. "Black? My little sister takes her coffee *black*?"

I glanced up at him, unsure what warranted the enthusiasm. "That's how I like it?"

"No way. You just don't know how to make it right. Here, I can fix this." He grabbed a clean mug and dumped equal amounts of coffee and creamer into it. He gave the mug a quick swirl and slid it towards me.

I picked it up and sniffed it skeptically; the drink was almost as white as I was. I took a small sip and almost barfed it back into the cup. It was sticky and sweet and didn't even taste like coffee.

"No thanks," I gagged, and shoved the mug back at him.

He took it with a grumble. "Who taught you how to drink coffee?"

I pondered that as I gratefully accepted the fresh mug Jayde handed to me. *Nic did.* I stared at the steaming brown liquid and managed a smile that felt genuine.

"How's your rib?" Mrs. Nolan's voice jerked me out of the pleasant memory.

I glared at her. "How did you know about that?"

"Ephesus told me," she said with a gesture in his direction.

I gripped the hot mug with both hands. "It's fine," I said, forcing the lie to sound placid and not bitter.

"I need to look at it." She took her plate to the sink and dropped it in the soapy water. "I want to make sure you don't have any fractures or internal bleeding, and I have some breathing exercises I want you to do. I can tell you're breathing shallowly, and if you do that too long, you'll get pneumonia."

I sucked in my breath involuntarily and was instantly reminded how much breathing *did* hurt.

She studied me. "Come to the infirmary after breakfast and I'll get you some pain medication."

That was definitely a bribe to get me to show up, and unfortunately, it would probably work. Thankfully Ephesus spared me the necessity of giving her a verbal reply by handing me a plate loaded with food. He gestured over to an empty table, and I followed, sliding onto the bench next to him.

He crammed a scoop of eggs into his mouth and then gestured at my plate with his fork. "Eat up. You need your strength."

"I promise I had three full meals yesterday." Eating didn't appeal to me—especially since swallowing *also* hurt—but I bravely stabbed the mound of nearly-white, gummy scrambled eggs and took a bite.

Jayde joined us at the table and set my tablet down in front of me. I frowned up at him; my tablet had been in my backpack, which I'd abandoned somewhere in the halls last night. Had he been digging in my stuff?

He put his hand up. "I just charged it." He took a sip of coffee. "And looked up who it was registered to."

I grabbed my device and self-consciously wiped his fingerprints off the screen with my sleeve. "You could have asked me."

He shrugged. "You were asleep."

"So you went digging in my purse?"

His jaw tensed, making his neck look even more muscular. "Look, keeping this place off the radar is a lot of work, so forgive me if I take digital security seriously."

Heat flashed across my cheeks, and I looked down at my plate.

He sat down across from me and leaned forward. "Hey, I'm just trying to keep everyone safe—including you."

"I know," I mumbled.

He leaned back and sighed. "I'm sorry to make you do this, but you can't keep that tablet here. All the internet traffic in the building is filtered, but it's not bulletproof. We can't have any activity from 'Andromeda' showing up on our log."

I looked up. "Can't I just take it offline?"

"That's even worse," Ephesus inserted. "If you go offline for large portions of the day, it will trip the algorithm."

Jayde nodded. "And I don't want the United to check your file and see that Andromeda takes the same bus route every day and then suspiciously drops offline when she reaches this address."

Ephesus tapped the screen. "I can set it up with a program that will run background activity all day—games, movies, that kind of thing. It will make it look like you're just hanging out at home for the summer."

"But…" The protest came to my lips and died. *But my Bible…*

"It will be safer if you leave it plugged in at the Vons'. Which, we need to talk about them." Ephesus put his fork down. "I think you should sleep at their house."

"What?" both Jayde and I protested at the same time.

Jayde was quicker to recover. "We need her here."

Who cares what you need? "I need to be here. Dad—"

Ephesus put a hand on my shoulder to stop me. "Phil, there's nothing you can do about Dad."

But it's my fault. "I—"

"He's right."

I looked up. Mrs. Nolan stood a respectful distance away, leaning against the counter, but she had clearly been listening. "There's nothing you can do about your father. We can't even begin to work on him until we get that tube unlocked, and even after he's thawed, he'll be in revival therapy for several weeks. There is literally nothing you can do but wait."

She met my eyes, and for the first time since yesterday, her expression was neither cold nor bitter. "I promise."

I looked away. Ephesus squeezed my shoulder. "And you'll be safer waiting at the Vons'."

"But what about you? I can't leave you."

"I promise I'm not going anywhere. Look, if my file wasn't a mess, I wouldn't be here either. But until I can safely get online, I have to stay off the grid."

I sat upright—a little too quickly. I concealed a wince. "I can fix your file. I bought you new prints."

Jayde's eyebrows formed a bright orange knot on his forehead. "From whom?"

"Andes," I said, and watched for a reaction.

His face relaxed. "How'd you get in? He told me he's not taking work anymore."

"I had a referral," I said, and for a brief moment felt powerful.

"Where'd you get money for prints?" Ephesus demanded.

I turned to him. "I have plenty of money. Thames—"

I caught sight of Mrs. Nolan in my peripheral and stopped.

Her expression darkened again. "No need to be ashamed of it. It's your money." She slammed her mug on the counter and walked out.

Ephesus watched her leave before turning back to me. "I take it you inherited more than their last name."

"Yeah, basically." I brushed off the uncomfortable emotions. "Point is, I bought new prints for you and Dad from Andes."

"So that's what you meant when you told Dad you arranged for his affairs. Was he supposed to meet Andes last night?"

"Yeah, but Andes said he never made it." My face numbed as the realization flooded me. "Carnegie must have intercepted him before he got there."

Memories of Carnegie's cruel laugh and final words rushed over me.

Oh, Philadelphia, you know this is all your fault, right?

"But how?" Jayde slapped a hand on the table. "Even I didn't know you'd been talking with Andes, or I'd have gotten there first."

That was hardly a comforting thought, but I knew the answer. "He was watching my file. He knew about Andromeda."

You led me right to him.

Carnegie was right: It was all my fault. He'd been following me the whole time; he'd seen me visit Andes. When he overheard me talking to Dad on the radio, he knew exactly what was going to happen. All he had to do was send men to watch Andes's shop. Dad walked right into their hands, because I led them there.

You should have stayed on Mars, sweetheart.

Ephesus slid his good arm around me, but I could barely feel it. *Oh Daddy, I'm so sorry.*

Ephesus rubbed my shoulder, as if that could coax some life back into me. "It's going to be okay. I'll just get my prints altered somewhere else."

"No, Andes is still your best bet," Jayde argued. "I can provide cover. There's a back way in. We'll go this afternoon."

I pulled away from Ephesus. "I'm going with you."

"Absolutely not. I'm taking you back to the Vons'."

"Ephesus, please—"

Jayde spoke over me. "I still think she should stay here."

"You don't get to decide," I snapped. "And I'm going to Andes's. I need to find out if that's what really happened—maybe he saw something." I looked into Ephesus's eyes and pleaded with him. "Please. I have to fix this."

He relented with a smile that was more sad than affectionate. "Okay."

My tablet flickered on, vibrating with a silent notification. I picked it up and saw a text from Stanyard.

GOT EVERYTHING CONFIGURED. GOING TO START RUNNING THE PROGRAM NOW

A prayer lifted some of the weight off my heart. *Thank you, Jesus. It's going to be okay.*

Ephesus leaned over to read the screen. "I'm going to go help him." He stood up and clasped my shoulder. "Please eat."

I grunted and forced myself to swallow another forkful of now-cold eggs. Ephesus grabbed his coffee cup and hurried out.

I sent Stanyard a thank you, then went back to methodically eating. I figured if I ate one bite at a time in a rhythm, I'd eventually get it all down.

Jayde watched me labor for a minute. "Do you want fresh coffee? It's probably cold by now."

"It's fine," I said, even though I took a sip and realized it wasn't.

He pushed his empty mug aside and leaned his arms on the table. "We need to talk."

I stabbed my toast with my fork, even though that was definitely not the recommended way to eat bread. *Do we have to do this now?*

"I know you're not a fan of the way I… followed you."

Just say it like it is. You stalked me. You stalked me, and you lied to me, and you almost got me killed.

"But the truth is, there's a lot going on. Stuff you don't know about—stuff your dad didn't tell you about."

I stopped when I remembered my dad's cold words on the radio.

Look, Blue Fire, there's more going on than you realize, things I can't discuss on here.

I looked up at Jayde.

His green eyes held mine. "Your dad isn't who he says he is. He's done this before."

"Done what?" I asked, but my tablet cut me off. I looked down to see another text from Stanyard.

YOU NEED TO GET UP HERE

5

I didn't bother to respond. I grabbed my tablet, swung my legs over the bench, and started running.

"What is it?" Jayde called.

"Dad!" I shouted as I darted out the door.

I ran to the elevator and back to the lab, ignoring the burning in my side. As I approached the window, I could see Stanyard and Ephesus standing over the tube. I felt a rush of hope soiled with fear. Had they cracked the password already? It couldn't have been that easy—could it?

I shoved the door open. Stanyard looked up and declared, "We have another problem."

"What now?" I gasped, out of breath from the sprint. I winced and braced myself against the doorframe, struggling not to drop my tablet.

Stanyard frowned at me but didn't comment. "It only lets us attempt the passcode three times before it locks us out for twenty-four hours."

He pointed at the control panel; it was glowing an angry red with an ominous counter ticking down. Ephesus stood with his back to me, glaring at the monitor.

Jayde jogged up behind me. "Didn't it warn you after the first two attempts?"

Stanyard flushed almost as red as the screen. "Yeah, but I missed it."

"How?" Jayde spat with absolutely no mercy.

Stanyard's eyes flittered around the room, looking anywhere but in my direction. "I had to patch my program to work with this OS, and I messed up the code for the warning relay."

Ephesus came to his defense. "We can adjust the program to space out the attempts so it doesn't trigger the lockout, but it won't do any good."

"Why not?" I burst, my last shred of hope imploding with the question.

Ephesus finally looked up at me. "Do you know how long it will take to try all of the possible potential passwords if we can only attempt one every five minutes?"

I wasn't good at math, but even I knew that it would take an eternity to crack the password at that pace. And time was one thing we didn't have.

All of Mrs. Nolan's warnings about Dad being under too long thundered in my skull.

Jayde took a minute to appreciate the gravity of that statement, then grunted. "Is there another way in?"

Ephesus grunted. "Yeah, but I don't like it. We could pry the casing off and try wiring into the machine directly. If we can find the right relays, we could bypass the computer and trigger the defrost procedure manually—but that's as good as killing him."

The gasp I made was involuntary. "Why?"

"Bringing him back to temperature is an incredibly delicate process. These machines are designed to run hundreds of diagnostics and adjust the procedure automatically based on how the body is responding." Ephesus rapped the monitor with his knuckles. "If we bypass the computer, we'd have to replicate all of that manually—and we won't have access to any of the sensor readouts."

"We'd not only need an incredibly skilled revival technician who can do everything by hand, but we'd also need a mechanic familiar with the tube design. And I don't know where we'd find either of those off the radar." Stanyard looked to Jayde.

Jayde shook his head, and I swallowed my heart.

"I can also try extracting the memory dump," Ephesus added, voice loud but devoid of any optimism. "There's no telling if that will work, but I can't even attempt it until tomorrow."

Stanyard dragged his hands through his already-matted hair. "Until then, I'd recommend collecting some educated guesses as to what Carnegie's code might have been. Randomized attempts aren't going to work."

It took me a minute to wade through the blinding fog of fear and realize that all three boys were staring at me.

"I hardly knew him... You worked with him longer." I turned pleading eyes to Ephesus.

He sighed. "Yeah, there's some things I can try—but it would be a lot easier if I were online."

Jayde took charge. "We need to get your prints fixed. I'll make the arrangements—we leave in an hour." He strode from the room without waiting for a response.

Stanyard waited until Jayde's footsteps faded down the hall before he turned to me. "I'm sorry, Phil."

I looked up and gave him a weak smile. "Thanks."

"No, I mean... *I'm* sorry. If I had known Carnegie had this password-protected..."

He heaved a sigh, his shoulders nearly caving in on themselves. I noted how pale his face was and how red his eyes were and realized he blamed himself.

"You had no way of knowing, man," Ephesus consoled him.

"I know!" Stanyard pinched his eyes shut. "But if I had, I would have—"

"Would have what?" I interrupted. "Let Carnegie shoot me instead?"

He opened his eyes and stared at me.

"You did what you had to do," I declared, as much for myself as for him.

His lips twitched.

"So what now?" Ephesus tapped the frosty glass. "I'll do some digging, but frankly, I'm not optimistic that I'll be able to find anything. Most of my time on Mars was spent on the wrong side of the door."

I knew exactly what that was like.

"Do we have any of the Wing 74 data left? Did any of Thames's servers survive the virus?" Stanyard suggested.

The obvious answer hit me with a wave of relief. "Nic!" I cried.

They both stopped and looked at me. I held up my tablet. "I can call Nic. He was Carnegie's boss—surely he has some of his old passcodes."

I unlocked my tablet and opened our encrypted messaging app. My pulse quickened as hope flowed through me. Nic would know what to do. He had a whole server's worth of data on Carnegie; surely he could find something. He could fix this...

After you tell him what you've done.

I hesitated with my finger over his profile picture. Nic had no idea what happened yesterday. Last he knew, I was lazing around his parents' house, waiting to hear from my dad. I was going to have to explain to Nic that I'd ignored every piece of advice he'd given me and nearly gotten us all killed.

I knew you wouldn't listen to Nic. I knew you couldn't sit still.

My palms left a sweaty smear on the back of the tablet. Nic had been right about everything, especially me.

Stanyard wheeled a desk chair over to me. "What's the matter, Phil?"

I gratefully sat down. "I'm going to have to tell Nic what happened."

"Why?" Ephesus sputtered. "He doesn't need to know the details. You don't owe him anything."

"I don't know, I just... feel like he deserves to know." I couldn't quantify the emotion; I couldn't quantify anything around the anxiety that suddenly swelled in my throat. I quickly clicked on Nic's profile and started an audio call before I could change my mind.

We all stayed silent while it rang once, twice, three times. I involuntarily let out my breath when he answered.

"Who died?" he asked as soon as he picked up.

I was so stunned that I almost forgot to acknowledge him. "Uh... what?"

"It's the middle of the night over here." He cleared the grogginess out of his throat. "So either you forgot to look up interplanetary time zones, or someone's dead."

The morbid accuracy of his assessment made me shudder. "Well, no one's dead yet—that's why I need your help."

There was a beat. "What happened?"

His tone shifted—firmer, quieter, as if he'd expected this all along. I flushed as my neck and ears started to burn.

Stanyard leaned towards the speaker. "I can explain if you want."

"Who's that?" Nic barked.

"Stanyard," I said, and wondered if he'd even remember who that was.

It took him a minute. "The kid?"

"Wow, specific," Stanyard muttered.

Nic was happy to clarify. "The one who abandoned you in the alley—"

"Yes, yes," I cut him off. "Ephesus is here too."

Nic swore.

"Love you too," Ephesus shouted from across the room.

"Well, this ought to be an excellent bedtime story." There was rustling on the other end of the line, as if Nic had gotten up and walked across the room. I heard a keyboard clacking. "Start from the beginning, Andromeda."

When I hesitated, he added, "And if you were thinking of holding anything back, let me remind you that this app encrypts calls."

"You said it wasn't bulletproof..." I mumbled.

"It's a risk I'm willing to take. Start talking."

I swallowed and obeyed, beginning when I dropped Cea off at the transit station yesterday. I omitted the gorier details, but there was no way to paint the story in any fashion that sounded heroic.

"Carnegie must have picked him up outside of Andes's," I admitted halfway through.

"Oh, I'm quite sure that's exactly what happened," Nic snapped with more anger in his voice than I'd heard in a long time. He hadn't been that angry with me since I'd broken into Wing 74.

I gripped my tablet, the apologies tumbling out before I could stop them. "I know, I'm sorry, I should have—"

"You should have waited to contact Andes until you had your father with you, like I *told* you to do!" Nic was shouting now.

Ephesus straightened. "Hey! Lay off of her."

Stanyard tried to help. "It's not her fault—"

"Would you just let me finish the story?" I cut them all off. I had to get through this before I started crying again.

I stumbled through the rest of the tale, ending with how Carnegie had frozen my father.

I paused, waiting to see if there would be any more scolding. Instead, there was silence.

"Where is Carnegie now?" Nic finally asked.

His voice had returned to normal, which relieved some of the tension in the room. My pulse slowed. "He's dead. Stanyard shot him."

"Well, at least that much is a happy ending. How'd the kid find you?"

"He knew about Andromeda—Mrs. Nolan told him."

There was a hacking cough, as if he'd tried to take a drink of water and regretted it. "Nolan? Well, that explains everything and nothing."

"I know." I let out my breath and didn't offer up any more explanation. Ephesus was right—I didn't owe him anything.

Nic didn't wait. "Well, let's see if we can't keep everyone else alive and thawed. Do you know what kind of cryoprotectant he used? Who's the tube manufacturer? Was it a controlled slow freeze, or did he vitrify him?"

I only knew what half of those words meant. I glanced at Ephesus.

"Hang on." He walked over to the terminal and started swiping through menus. "Looks like a Kaylon Core brand... model FM-2030."

I heard typing on Nic's side of the line. "It definitely wasn't a 'slow freeze,'" I offered. "It happened almost instantly." I rubbed my arm and hoped he wouldn't ask for a more detailed description of the process.

"I've got a schematic for the makeup of the cryoprotectant here," Ephesus said. "It looks like it's dimethyl sulfoxide based..."

Nic swore, and I knew we were in trouble.

"No need," he muttered. "That model number tells me all I need to know."

I swallowed until I had enough courage to ask, "What do *I* need to know?"

"Because I don't hate you, I'm going to give it to you straight." He gave me only a beat to prepare myself before he declared, "I don't think your father is coming back."

The boys were graciously silent while I came up with a million excuses as to why he was wrong. "Mrs. Nolan said he was going to need some skin grafts and a blood transfusion..."

"He's going to need a lot more than fresh blood if he's going to breathe again," Nic snapped, then sighed. "Listen, Andi, that tube wasn't designed to preserve people for revival. It was designed to preserve people for harvesting."

I reflexively looked at my father's petrified face.

"Preserving people for revival is a *process*. You need to prep the body, replace some of the fluids with inert gases—you can't just flash-freeze them. The amount of tissue and organ damage that causes is astronomical."

"But that doesn't make any sense," I cried. "Carnegie needed my father."

"He needed his *brain*."

Everything dropped to the pit of my stomach.

Nic continued, more slowly this time. "All he needed was the formula for Red Rain—which is in your father's memory banks somewhere, or at least the pieces needed to reconstruct it. He could have easily hooked your father's brain to a computer and transferred a lot of the data—that's at least real science. Or—never mind."

He cut off with a grunt. Every fiber of my being told me I shouldn't ask, but I did anyway. "Or what?"

He mumbled under his breath before answering. "Or he could have thawed your father and kept him in a vegetative state. That's the economical option. All he would have had to do was feed your father key images or words, and the brain would have supplied the needed memories. Any old synaptic device could read them. Your father wouldn't have to be 'viable' for that to work—it's all subconscious."

I turned to Ephesus, silently begging him to tell me it wasn't true, but he'd washed as white as a sheet. We both knew what method Carnegie would have chosen. Stanyard breathed a frantic prayer.

A cold tear slid down my cheek. "What do I do?" I whispered.

"Start making funeral arrangements?" Nic barked, then caught himself. "Look—I won't tell you not to try. Kaylon is a legit company, and their equipment is state of the art. If you have any hope, it's going to be in the quality of their materials. But you're going to need a wickedly good revival technician."

Where was I going to find one of those? Jayde said he was going to make some calls, but he himself admitted his contact wasn't skilled. Even if we could find someone willing to do a very expensive procedure off the record, would they be good enough? What if my father died simply because we botched the procedure?

I would never forgive myself.

"I'm going back to bed now," Nic said when he realized I didn't have anything else to contribute.

"Wait," Stanyard called. "There is one thing you can help us with."

"Yeah?"

"Carnegie password-locked the cryotube. We can't even begin to thaw it out until we crack it, and so far hacking has only triggered security lockouts. Do you have any idea what he might have used for a passcode? Any common codes he's used before?"

"At 3 am I don't know anything. But in the morning I'll start digging around in his files and see what I can find."

"Thank you," I offered with as much sincerity as I could around the gathering tears.

He hesitated. "Of course," he said, and hung up.

6

There was silence in the lab except for the humming of the machines. I sat there, barely breathing, feeling like I could cry but that the tears were just out of reach. My sinuses were clogged with emotion, like the apologies and guilt and shame were frozen in there.

Frozen and unviable. Just like Dad.

Stanyard was the first to speak. "Phil, I'm so sorry." He reached a hand towards my shoulder, then caught himself. He quickly stepped back.

Ephesus walked over to me. He knelt beside the chair and wrapped his good arm around me. I buried my face in his shoulder, willing myself to cry, apologize, *something*.

Only one thought solidified. "He's dead, isn't he?"

Ephesus didn't answer. I felt his shoulders tense.

I pulled away. "Daddy's dead."

And I killed him.

"No," Ephesus said, but not quickly enough.

Stanyard tried to cover for him, voice artificially loud. "There's still hope. Even Nic said there's a chance, and he is not known for his optimism."

"He just said that to make me feel better," I muttered, even though Nic had literally never made any effort to make me feel better about anything.

"I don't think so." Ephesus tapped the darkened screen of my tablet. "Nic has a lot of vices, but I don't think he's lying to you."

A tiny sliver of warmth crawled into my soul when I realized he was right. Nic would lie about a lot of things to a lot of people, but he wouldn't lie to me. Not anymore.

Ephesus stood up. "We need to find a revival technician—which means I need to get online and make some calls. I'm going to go find Jayde and see if he's ready."

I nodded. "I'll go find my backpack."

"What you need to find is a shower—and a change of clothes." Ephesus wrinkled his nose at me.

I should have been offended, but a glance down at myself proved he was right. I'd nearly died in this outfit, and you could tell.

"I'm sure Mrs. Nolan has something you can borrow," Stanyard offered.

I grimaced. I did not relish the idea of sharing clothes with Mrs. Nolan, but I didn't have much of a choice. I couldn't go to Andes's looking like this.

"Fine," I relinquished, "but don't leave without me."

Ephesus led me to the girls' locker room and left me to it. It was probably the most degrading shower I'd ever taken; the tile floor was freezing, and the generic soap they had in the dispenser on the wall smelled like a hospital. But I'd rather smell like a hospital than reek of death and terror.

I emerged to find a pile of toiletries on the bench. Someone had left a comb, deodorant, and a toothbrush, along with an oversized gray hoodie. It didn't look like anything Mrs. Nolan would wear, but at least it was clean. I sponged out my jeans, whipped my hair into a stubby braid, and brushed my teeth. I pulled the hoodie over my head and instantly felt more human; it was thick and soft, and I could hide my arms inside it like a hug.

Jayde was waiting for me outside. "Let's roll."

Lev, the young Russian I'd met yesterday, and a burly soldier twice his size accompanied us. We piled into a giant black SUV, the kind bad guys in movies drove. Jayde did, in fact, know a back way into Andes's; we parked at an abandoned warehouse two blocks away and entered through the alley. The precaution felt unnecessary, however; with three heavily-armed military guys accompanying us, we probably could have just gone through the front.

"Lass! You're all right!" Andes's booming voice filled the shop as soon as we entered. Thankfully he didn't have any other customers. He strode up to me, blithely ignoring the men, and grasped my hand in both of his. "Don't you know it's rude to hang up on a man like that?"

"I'm sorry, there was a mishap. But I've brought you some work." I gestured at Ephesus.

Andes released me and turned to size Ephesus up. "You must be the lucky lad!" He offered his tattooed hand, then pulled it back when he realized Ephesus's dominant hand was in a cast. "Have we met?"

"Not in the flesh." Ephesus stepped forward and whispered something in Andes's ear.

Andes's face split in a grin. "Klez! Well, isn't this my lucky day."

I glanced between them. "You two know each other?"

"Everyone's heard of Klez. Best coder in Boston." Andes slapped him on the back, a gesture which both looked and sounded painful.

Ephesus covered a wince. "That's hyperbole, but thank you."

Andes opened his mouth to say something else, then stopped. His eyes and face darkened like a storm had blown over the moor. "But if you're Klez, then that makes you..." His finger drifted to me.

Jayde stepped up. "This is Blue Fire."

Andes grunted something that wasn't English, but it definitely didn't sound polite. "I take it my no-call, no-show from last night was Catalyst." He spat out my dad's callsign like it was a piece of unchewable food.

"Yes," I admitted with a swallow.

Andes rubbed the bulging veins in his temples. "Why didn't you tell me?"

"It was none of your business." I glared at Jayde.

"Lass, I know you're new here, but let me teach you some etiquette about dealing outside the law." Andes crossed his arms over his thick chest and frowned at me. "When your client is on the United's ten most wanted, it's customary to let people know what they're getting into."

Desperation burst in my mind, but then I remembered that I was the one with the money. I held the power in this relationship.

I straightened and pulled my shoulders back. "If you're not confident enough to handle my case, then I'll take my business elsewhere."

The glitter returned to his eyes. "Oh no, I know where my loyalties lie."

He pulled the collar of his shirt down to reveal a tattoo below his right clavicle. It was a mystical-looking bird with a lightning bolt clutched in his talons—the same tattoo Cea had on the inside of her arm.

I searched his face. The image meant nothing to me, but if both Andes and Cea had one, it must be important. It probably meant both of them were part of the same sect in the underground. Cea was someone I still trusted, so hopefully that meant I could still trust Andes, too.

"Glad to hear it," I said.

He adjusted his shirt and glanced at Ephesus. "We need to get you fixed up—follow me."

He led us into one of the private booths off the lobby. Shoving the table aside, he reached up and pushed on a ceiling tile, revealing a metal ladder. With one yank, he pulled it down. He gestured at me. "Ladies first."

I glanced at Ephesus, who nodded. I grabbed the rungs and hurried up.

Above the ceiling was a glittering lab that looked like it belonged in the base on Mars. Overhead fluorescents drowned the room in sterile light. A dozen shiny machines competed for floorspace, and the air thrummed with electricity. In the middle of it all was an exam table that looked like a prop from the torture bay in a bad movie. The only thing not metal in the whole room were the brick walls, which lent a strange steampunk vibe to the space.

The rest of the group joined me. "I thought you said you were out of business," Jayde groused.

Andes pulled the ladder up behind us. "I never said I was out of business. I just said I wouldn't work for your prices." He pointed at a chair in the corner. "You, sit."

Ephesus obeyed, and Andes went about prepping a machine that looked exactly like the one the technician on Mars had used when I'd gotten my prints altered.

"Dare I ask what happened to Catalyst last night?" Andes glanced over his shoulder at me as he worked.

I took a deep breath. "Actually, I was hoping you could tell me."

I gave him a simplified version of the story, saying only that we believed an enemy had gotten to Dad first. Andes didn't need to know specifics.

He let out a growl from deep in his throat. "I'm afraid I can't help you. He called to make an appointment for 7 pm, but he never showed. I kept the shop open all night, but when you called and seemed as surprised as I was that he wasn't there—I assumed something had gone wrong."

He rolled the laser arm over to the chair. He eyed Ephesus's cast disdainfully. "This is gonna hurt, lad."

He took Ephesus's broken arm out of the sling and carefully bent it so that it was flat on the arm of the chair. Then he started sliding Ephesus's fingers into the clamps that would hold them still for the procedure. Ephesus did his best to swallow a wince.

Once he had Ephesus strapped down, Andes pulled a chair over to the computer terminal and started typing. "I'm sorry, lass. If there's any word on the street, I'll let you know. But if the United got ahold of him—I wouldn't be optimistic."

"I know." I wasn't optimistic anyway, but for once the government was not the cause of my misery.

He ignored me to focus on his work. I knew from experience that the procedure would take several hours, so I amused myself by wandering around the shop. Jayde, Lev, and their partner settled in chairs by the exit and engaged in a whispered conversation that apparently didn't involve me, which was just as well.

I found a binder of tattoo designs on a table and started flipping through it. They were all print-outs—pixelated ones at that, like they'd been run on an old copier—probably because the images were too sensitive to be stored on a computer. The first few pages were filled with flags and national symbols, emblems the United had long since branded as illegal. I lingered on a sketch of the American flag, a banner I had never seen fly in real life. Even my father was too young to remember when the United States was truly free.

I kept looking. The designs got progressively more seditious: crosses, the star of David, the Muslim crescent and star. There were words in foreign languages and symbols that looked like code. And there it was again—that bird with the thunderbolt.

I traced the image with my finger, wondering what it meant. I thought about asking, but Andes had his nose to the screen, editing one of Ephesus's prints.

I turned the page to find a picture of a brain. It was far too complex to be a tattoo; it looked more like a schematic, with annotations and arrows crisscrossing the neural pathways.

The next few pages were more of the same. There were markups of brains, lungs, even kidneys. And then I came to a sketch for an artificial heart.

That's definitely what it was, and an advanced one at that. I skimmed the list of features and remembered Mrs. Nolan's words.

He'll lose most of his organs. He'll need more transplants...

"Andes... do you do organ transplants?"

He didn't look up from his work. "I don't, but I know someone who does. Why, you need something done?"

Oh Jesus, please let it be.

I kept testing the waters. "And what about a skin grafter?"

He glanced back at me and arched an eyebrow.

I sighed and tossed the binder on the table. "I need a revivalist—and a good one."

The soldiers stopped talking and watched.

Andes punched a button on the machine to pause the procedure. He swiveled his chair around to face me and planted his hands on his knees. "I think you'd better tell me the whole story—from the beginning."

I looked to Ephesus, who gave me a subtle nod.

So I told Andes the truth—how "Catalyst" was back at base, frozen in a block of ice. When I was done, Andes reached up to massage the veins in his temples, which were even more swollen than before.

"You know how I said you should disclose all the relevant details about your clients? *That* was a relevant detail."

I shrugged. "Can you do it?"

He sighed. "Yes, we can."

Hope raged through me. *Thank you, Jesus!* I shared an eager look with Ephesus, who mouthed praises.

Andes cut off our celebration with a flick of his finger. "But I'm warning you, it will not be pretty. We've worked with that brand of cryogenics before—it's not the first time we've brought back someone the government iced. But it's a very harsh process, and we'll have no idea how badly he's been damaged until we get in there."

"I know," I said, even as my soul squeezed.

"And if you're wanting to do this all under the radar, you're going to have to take what you can get when it comes to replacement body parts. I can't guarantee that his skin will be all the same color when we're done."

The thought of my father being stitched together like a puppet made me want to throw up, but I fought the feeling down. "I understand—just get it done."

He studied me. "It's going to cost a fortune."

"I don't care."

"*How* much is this going to be?" Jayde asked.

"It's fine," I snapped, and realized I sounded exactly like Nic.

Andes was still watching me. "And one more thing—I guarantee you he'll suffer some memory loss."

I swallowed. "How much?"

He didn't sugarcoat it. "I've seen all ends of the spectrum."

I thought of the Vons and flinched. What if Dad ended up exactly like Nic's parents—barely able to take care of himself? What if he didn't remember Ephesus? What if he didn't remember me?

I pinched my eyes shut. It didn't matter. I couldn't give up on Dad. I had to fix what I'd done, and if that meant spending every penny and walking with him through therapy for three years, so be it.

I breathed through my nose until the anxiety subsided. I opened my eyes and met Andes's stare. "You're hired."

7

Ephesus insisted I get home to the Vons before dark. After we got back to base and checked on Dad, he gave me a tight one-armed hug and promised he would call me immediately if there was any change. I couldn't bring myself to tell him goodbye; I was choking on the irrational fear that as soon as I walked away, he would disappear from my life again. I knew it was ridiculous, and that we were all as safe as possible given the circumstances, but my emotions had long since abandoned reason.

Stanyard respected my need for silence as he drove me home. He parked in front of the Vons' house and turned to me. "I'll come pick you up at nine tomorrow."

"Thanks," I whispered, and got out. He idled on the road until I disappeared around the back of the house.

I let myself in the back door with my key and was instantly met by screeching.

"Where in the world have you been?"

I looked up into the flushed face of Mrs. Von. She blocked the hall, feet apart and hands on her hips. She made a grand attempt to leer over me, even though she was about an inch shorter.

"Where have you been?" she repeated, using language that would have made Nic proud.

While "a secret rebel base across town" would have been the truthful answer, I had a feeling that wasn't the answer I should give her.

Unsurprisingly, she didn't wait for an explanation. "You were gone all night, and when I went up to check your room, your suitcase was packed... What was I supposed to think?"

I gaped at her. I hadn't expected her to even notice I was missing. "I'm sorry, I—"

"Is that her?" Mr. Von called from the kitchen.

"Yes, finally," Mrs. Von muttered, and I realized that was the closest to an "I was worried about you" that I'd get from her.

Mr. Von was a little more obvious with his affection. He ran out into the hall and embraced me. "I'm so glad you're safe. When you didn't show up for breakfast..."

I connected the dots. I'd broken the pattern by disappearing, and it had sent their fragile minds into a tailspin. I returned Mr. Von's hug, ignoring the pain in my ribs. "I'm sorry, I was sleeping over at a friend's house. I thought I mentioned it..." I stepped back and gave Mrs. Von a sheepish shrug and smile. "It won't happen again."

She accepted the penance. "Well, I'm glad I didn't call the police."

I flinched. *Me too.* The last thing I needed was the police out looking for Andromeda.

"Well, you're just in time for dinner!" Mr. Von, evidently fully recovered, led the way back to the kitchen. "We're having... what are you making again, dear?"

Mrs. Von threw up her hands. "I don't even know anymore." The order in her universe had been restored, and now she just looked exhausted.

I took a bold risk and lightly touched her arm. "I'll finish cooking."

She eyed me for a minute, then smiled.

Even I couldn't figure out what Mrs. Von had been trying to make, but thankfully it wasn't that hard to retrofit the half-browned ground beef into another recipe. After dinner, I let Mr. Von talk me into watching two episodes of his current sitcom; I wasn't in the mood for TV, but I felt like I owed it to him.

After I finally excused myself, I went upstairs to take a longer, more satisfying shower. I threw every stitch of clothing in the wash and took my time scrubbing my fingernails and treating my scratches with antibiotic cream.

By the time I was done, my rib was in agony. I looked in the mirror and traced the giant welt on my side; it was already starting to turn a horrid shade of purple. I'd avoided going to see Mrs. Nolan earlier in the day—and had surprisingly gotten away with it—but now I was regretting not getting pain medication. I raided some ibuprofen I found in the bathroom cabinet and prayed it would take the edge off.

I went back to Cea's room and took my tablet off the charger. The notifications informed me that Ephesus had added me as a contact and reminded me to ask Nic about the password.

I sat down on the edge of the bed and sent Nic a message.

DID YOU FIND ANY PASSCODES?

The response was instantaneous.

CALL ME

I rolled my eyes and did as I was told, starting an audio call.
"Where are you?" he barked.

I sighed. Nic wasn't one to start conversations with hello, but the least he could do was not yell at me. "At your parents' house."

"Good." A popup appeared prompting me to enable video.

I stared at the screen in surprise. *Why…?* I hit accept. My video flickered on, and I realized I was nowhere in frame. I tried to lean back against the headboard and managed to pinch my bruised side. A cry of pain left my lips before I could filter the sound.

"Did he hurt you?"

"Huh?" I managed as I blinked away the flashing colors.

"Carnegie. Did he hurt you?"

I started to say "I'm fine," then realized I was tired of saying that. "He kicked me in the ribs."

Nic didn't answer. I looked down to find him glaring at the camera. "Andromeda," he said finally.

I couldn't read his tone of voice, but he didn't sound happy. I glanced away as my cheeks began to burn again. "Look, can we not do this? I know what you're going to say… I should have come back to Mars with Cea."

"The door's still open."

I looked back down at the screen.

He sighed and leaned back in his desk chair. "What's the plan?"

I carefully propped a pillow against my injured side and settled against the headboard. "Andes thinks his people can do it. They've worked with this kind of preservation before. He says Dad might suffer some memory loss, but almost everything else is replaceable."

I tried not to dwell on the fact that Dad might end up like Nic's parents—or with a body frankensteined from parts not his own.

"How much is that going to cost?"

My head was aching too much for me to remember numbers. "I don't know—a lot."

"Do you need money?"

My face flushed again, this time for a completely different reason. I brushed past the comment. "I don't owe him anything until we get the tube unlocked. Did you find anything?" I shoved the ball back in his court and hoped he would do the talking for a while.

"Yes, I'm going to send you a list of all the passwords I could retrieve from the database." His finger danced across the screen as he swiped through menus in the background. "He left some personal devices here—I'll try searching those tomorrow. But I have to warn you that Carnegie was not the type to reuse passwords."

I acknowledged that with a groan. "Any better ideas?"

"None worth mentioning. But I do know that if it's possible to hack around it, your brother will figure it out."

I realized that was the best compliment Nic had ever paid my brother and smiled.

"When are you coming home?"

The question startled me. "You mean to Mars?"

He rubbed his forehead. "Do you have another permanent residence I'm not aware of?"

Do I have anywhere else to call home? It was a meta question I was definitely not capable of processing right now. "I... I don't know. I can't transport Dad while he's frozen."

"Actually you can," he grunted. "But regrettably, I don't know any revivalists on Mars."

The thought of packing everything up and running back to Mars was tempting, but I needed Andes's help. "I guess as soon as Dad's revived we'll come." *That's if Dad survives the process.*

"I'd recommend leaving as soon as he's viable, even if he's still in physical therapy. As long as he's stable enough to make the trip, we can fix the rest when you get here. I'd recommend you book separate flights—all of you are wanted by the law, and their files are shoddier than yours. If one of you trips a censor, you don't want all three of you to get caught..."

His words blurred together. I dropped the tablet on the bed and pinched my temples. He was asking me to make adult decisions about a reality I couldn't even fathom yet. I was exhausted and in pain and had a growing headache; I couldn't wrap my mind around tomorrow, let alone a few weeks from now.

It took me a minute to realize he'd stopped talking. "I'm sorry, Andi."

"What?" I mumbled, not caring that I wasn't in frame.

"I'm sorry about your father."

I let his tone of voice sink into me. "I know you are."

"Make sure you get at least eight hours of sleep and keep your calorie intake up. You should probably start doing some stretches and breathing exercises so you don't get a deflated lung…"

I groaned. Now he sounded like Mrs. Nolan. "Fine, I get it, Dad," I sassed, and then instantly regretted it. It was a cruel joke to make when my own father was dying in a block of ice.

What's gotten into you?

Nic didn't respond for a long moment. "Call me tomorrow night with an update."

It wasn't a suggestion. "Yessir," I promised.

There was another beat, and then he hung up.

I shoved my tablet aside and turned the lamp off. Gingerly, I slid under the covers, but it took me only seconds to realize that lying down was too painful. I nested myself in the pillows until I was partially propped up and marginally comfortable. The ibuprofen was working, sort of, at least enough that I could breathe without wincing.

I looked up at the darkened ceiling and suddenly realized that it was quiet—too quiet. I was alone, again, and I knew exactly what nightmares would await me as soon as I fell asleep.

My eyes started burning, but they were dry. I needed to cry, or pray, or something. Anything but this precarious waffling between life and death.

"Jesus, please… I need you."

I waited for the rush of peace that usually followed prayer, but it never came. I couldn't feel Him there, or anything at all. All I could sense was the block of grief that seemed to have permanently replaced the air in my lungs.

I tried again. "God, I'm sorry."

I know it's my fault.

"I'm so sorry… Please help me. I have to fix this."

Nothing changed. The silence was terrifying.

I fumbled for my tablet and turned it on, desperate for some noise. I took my device offline, then searched Nic's music archive until I found an old worship album. I could only hope the lyrics would fill the void where I could not.

I hit play and tossed my tablet towards the end of the bed. Pulling the blanket up to my chin, I closed my eyes and waited for darkness to come.

8

Mrs. Von almost didn't let me out the door in the morning.

"What time will you be home?" She stood in the middle of the entryway, arms crossed.

"Before dinner, I promise." I tried to sidle past her; Stanyard was already waiting for me.

Mrs. Von sidestepped to make my exit impossible. "I said what *time*."

I sighed. "Five o'clock."

She nodded curtly. "All right. And watch your attitude, young lady."

I swallowed. "Yes ma'am, sorry ma'am. I promise—it's just a school project."

She wasn't buying it, although whether that was because it was a bad lie or because I was a poor liar, I couldn't tell. "Well, make sure you keep your device on you. If you're a minute late, I'm calling you."

"Yes ma'am, I will." It was another lie. I wouldn't have my device on me; Jayde said I couldn't have any registered electronics on base. My tablet was up in Cea's room, charging;

Ephesus had installed a program that would simulate innocuous activity all day.

I wasn't thrilled about leaving it behind; I felt naked walking out without my device, my too-light backpack slipping off my shoulders. But I knew it was safer this way. Besides, Mrs. Von wouldn't even know how to call me if she wanted to; I hadn't given her my number, not that she'd remember it if I did.

She finally stepped back and let me reach the door. I darted out onto the porch before she could change her mind. "I'll see you tonight!" I called with artificial cheerfulness.

She loomed in the doorway. "Who's that?" She jabbed her finger at Stanyard's car.

"A classmate," I answered, which was surprisingly not a lie.

Stanyard rolled down the window and waved. "Hi, Mrs. Von Nieuwenhuyse."

She did not return the greeting.

I slid into the passenger seat and quickly put the window up. "I have to be home by five, or she's calling CPS."

He chuckled as he pulled away from the curb. "They must really care about you."

I processed that. "Yeah, I guess you're right." *Thank you, Jesus.*

"Did you sleep okay?"

"Yeah," I fudged, and hoped I wasn't about to be interrogated. I'd gotten plenty of sleep; the problem was what I dreamed about while I was under. "And I swear I ate all my breakfast."

That seemed to satisfy his minimum requirements. He braked at the end of the street and twisted around to grab something out of the backseat. "I brought you something."

I turned to him and tried to figure out why the idea of him giving me gifts made me nervous.

He set a book in my lap.

A Bible.

A real, paper Bible. A muttered exclamation left my lips as I picked it up.

It was beautiful. It was black leather-bound, with a gold cross and the initials *EMH* embossed on the cover. It was in excellent condition, with only a little creasing on the spine and a trickle of water damage on the corner.

I looked up at him. "Where in the world did you get this?"

He grinned. "There's a black market for everything." He turned his eyes back to the road. "I knew you had to leave your tablet behind, and, well... I know how you get when you don't have your reader."

I flushed. There was no denying it, but I was surprised Stanyard had noticed. I'd never talked books with him, not even when we were children. That's what I had my girlfriend Cami and Stanyard's sister Mira for.

Unless Stanyard had been listening the whole time.

I pressed the book to my chest. "Thank you," I said, which seemed wholly inadequate to express my gratitude. I had a Bible again—and not only that, but a *physical* copy. I hadn't seen a paper Bible in years.

I opened it. According to the inscription, it had been gifted to someone's "Favorite Auntie" in the 2050s. Whoever the owner was had methodically filled the margins with penciled notes and multicolored highlighting. I fanned through the pages, breathing in the smell of aged paper and skimming the annotations filled with faith and hope.

I stopped when I came to Ephesians. The highlighting was heavier here, as if she'd been over the book multiple times. I settled on chapter one and started reading.

For our struggle is not against flesh and blood, but against the rulers, against the authorities, against the powers of this dark world...

I had finished the book and started Philippians before I realized I'd been reading in silence for the past twenty minutes, completely ignoring Stanyard. I glanced at him out of the corner of my eye and wondered if I should apologize.

He was watching the road, smiling.

Ephesus and Jayde met us as soon as we got in the building. Ephesus welcomed me with a hug. "You look better."

I felt better, probably because I'd just spent the last half-hour reading a physical Bible. "Any luck dumping the memory?"

He scratched his buzzed head. "It's called extracting the memory dump, and I hope so. I whipped up a program that should help, but I can't try it until the lockout releases here in a half hour."

"We should get on it," Stanyard said, and led the way towards the elevator.

I started to follow him. "I'm coming with you."

Ephesus stuck his arm out to stop me. "Oh no you're not. You're going to see Mrs. Nolan."

I grimaced. "I'm fine."

"I don't care. I got an earful this morning because you apparently never got checked out yesterday, and I'm not in the mood for another scolding. I promise I'll come get you if there's any progress."

"But—"

He ignored me and looked over my head at Jayde. "Make sure she gets there."

I turned to Jayde with a scowl I hoped was threatening. "Don't you dare."

He rubbed his neck and waited until Ephesus and Stanyard had disappeared in the elevator. "If you want... I could conveniently come up with new 'orders' for you. Despite what he thinks, I am in charge around here."

I let out my breath. "Please."

He jerked his head and led the way. I followed him to an elevator at the opposite end of the hall. We stepped in, and he called B3. According to the keypad, there were at least four subfloors beneath the ground level, making me wonder just how deep the building went.

"Where'd you get this building?" I asked as we descended.

"We acquired it when the company that used to own it went out of business. A benefactor 'bought them out,' and now we use all their infrastructure as a shell." He tapped the floor of the elevator, where the company's faded logo was printed on the scuffed linoleum.

I put the pieces together. "So the government thinks the company is still in operation?"

He nodded. "I have a dozen full-time people whose sole job it is to keep this place clean on paper."

The elevator dinged, and I followed him out into the hall. "How many people work for you?"

"I've got a troop of about a hundred that report directly to me, but there's several other lieutenants that work out of this building." As if reinforcing his statement, his phone beeped. He pulled it out of the pocket of his cargo pants and swiped through notifications.

I glanced around the dank hallway and tried to reconcile that information with what Cea and Stanyard had told me. "Stanyard said the underground was just an informal network of sympathizers."

"For him, it is." Jayde didn't look up from his device as he continued to walk and talk. "People like Stanyard and Andes are civilians. They have day jobs and help on their own terms. But for people like me and Lev, this is our life."

I recalled the day we'd met in Thames's office. "So when you hired yourself out to Thames…"

"Wasn't the first time I played double-agent, and it won't be the last." He pocketed his device and looked up at me. "Resistance isn't a hobby for me. And it shouldn't be for you either."

My skin prickled. "What?"

He didn't clarify. "We're here." He paused at a thick steel door and swiped his thumb on the keypad. He held the door open for me, and I reluctantly stepped inside.

Beyond was a cavernous room the size of a gymnasium. It was long and narrow and made entirely of concrete. The front of the room was sectioned into booths by steel dividers. At the far end, the floor and ceiling met in a sharp V, like the whole room was a funnel. Tracks ran the entire length of the ceiling, and from them hung targets of various sizes, all laced with bullet holes.

Suddenly, I knew where we were, and my stomach tried to cram itself up my throat.

Oh no, I can't—

"Here, put these in." Jayde dropped a pair of earbuds into my hand. They were so tiny and smooth that I feared they'd fall into my ear.

"Jayde, I don't—"

"Unless you want to go deaf, put them in." He popped his own pair in. "You'll still be able to hear me."

I shrugged my backpack off. With shaking hands, I slid the plugs into my ears and discovered he was right. I could no longer hear the echoing of our footsteps, which was incredibly disorienting, but his voice came through clearly.

"You need to learn to shoot." He pulled his pistol from his belt and pressed it into my hands.

I stared at the cold, heavy weapon and wondered if I'd rather go see Mrs. Nolan.

"Jayde, I don't know if I can—"

"Blue Fire," he snapped, and I flinched. "Stanyard and I aren't always going to be around to protect you. I can't have you out there on the streets unable to defend yourself."

The gun shook in my hands, and that's when I realized my whole body was trembling. *But I can't shoot people. I can't… kill.*

He studied me, and his voice softened. "Think of how differently things might have gone if you'd had a gun when you met Carnegie."

My throat clenched shut. He was right—I might have been able to save my dad had I been armed, or stronger, or more aware of my surroundings, or *something*, anything.

You could have prevented this.

I took a breath that sounded more like a gasp and wrapped my sweaty fingers around the gun. I pointed it straight ahead and cupped the hilt in my palm, just like I'd seen Cea and Stanyard do.

"First rule of gun safety—don't point unless you're prepared to shoot." Jayde pushed the barrel of the pistol down with his finger. "Point down."

"Right, sorry," I mumbled. My voice sounded disembodied through the earbuds, like I was having an out-of-body experience.

He spun me around to face the range. "For now, just practice shooting in the right direction. Aim for the slit in the bullet trap." He pointed at the funnel at the end of the room.

I nodded and stationed myself in one of the booths.

"Feet apart and put your right foot slightly back."

I obeyed, my sneakers sliding on the floor.

"Bend your knees and lean forward slightly." He demonstrated.

I tried to mimic him, but I felt clumsy and unstable. My knees were still shaking, and I looked more like a newborn calf than a fighter.

"Both hands on the hilt. Keep your finger off the trigger until you're ready."

I'll never be ready. I gripped the hilt, but the metal felt cold and slippery in my hands.

I can't do this.

"Remember, shoot for the wall." He took a step back. "Ready, aim, fire."

I didn't move my finger. "Are these real bullets?"

He arched an eyebrow. "I said *fire.*"

Oh God, help, I prayed, and squeezed the trigger.

I could barely hear the explosion, but the recoil sent shockwaves through my arm. I dropped the gun and stumbled back, yelling when my bruised side protested.

You shouldn't be doing this.

Jayde retrieved the gun and put it back in my hands. "Again."

"Jayde, I—"

"Again."

I winced and put myself in position. I tried to brace myself physically and emotionally, but it didn't soften the blow. I didn't drop the gun this time, but my rib absorbed the brunt of the force. I bit down on my tongue to keep from gasping. My eyes started to water as I forced myself to do it again and again. It was a good thing I wasn't trying to hit a particular target.

The muffled explosions echoed in my ears, and I tried not to think about the fact that each bullet fired could have ended a life.

It's fine, it's just a wall, no one's getting hurt...

I expended the bullets in the chamber and handed the gun back to Jayde. *There, you happy?*

He pulled a fresh clip from his belt, snapped it in the weapon, and held it out.

I groaned. My fingers were cramped, and I was sweating profusely. My ears rang in tune with my headache.

He wiggled the hilt. "You want to do this? You have to learn to be like us."

I took a step back. "But I don't want to do this. I'm not like you."

He grabbed my wrist and shoved the gun into my palm. "You will be."

I opened my mouth to argue, but a slamming door interrupted me. "What in the world are you doing?"

I turned. Mrs. Nolan stood in the doorway. "You should not be shooting."

For once, I completely agreed with her.

Jayde was undeterred. "She needs to learn."

"Not while she's got a bruised rib she doesn't." She dropped her medical bag on the floor.

I eagerly let go of the gun and backed away. Jayde's jaw tensed, but Mrs. Nolan cut him off before he could formulate words. "No. She needs to rest. Now you get out of my way and let me do my job, or I'm taking her home right now."

Jayde sized her up and wisely decided not to pick a fight. "Fine. You'll practice more tomorrow." He glared at me, as if I had any say in what was going on.

"She'll practice when I say she's well enough to practice."

Jayde didn't acknowledge the comment. He holstered his gun and strode out of the room.

Mrs. Nolan waited until his footsteps faded down the hall before she turned her frown on me. "You were supposed to come see me yesterday."

I put on a brave face as I took the earbuds out and put them in my pocket. "I felt fine."

"I can tell by the pace of your breathing that that's not true."

I made a concentrated effort to take a slow, deep breath. "I just pushed myself too hard, that's all."

That wasn't a lie, but she didn't buy it. "I need to make sure nothing's fractured." She bent and unzipped her medical bag.

I was pretty confident nothing was fractured; it didn't hurt *that* badly. "It's just a bruise, I checked. It'll heal on its own in a few days."

"Just let me scan you to be safe." She produced a small med scanner from her bag. It looked like an oversized digital thermometer with a bulky display. "The last thing you need is a punctured lung. Now come here."

She held out her hand. I took a step back.

"Andromeda," she said in the same tone of voice one might use with a toddler. "What is wrong with you? You were never like this before. You used to be such a polite girl."

My blood boiled. "Yeah, well, a lot has happened since we last met."

She let all her frustrations out in a sigh. "Andromeda, I'm only trying to help you."

"That's exactly what your husband said," I snapped.

She winced, and I almost took it back. *No—I'm tired of lying about how I feel.* If she wanted the truth, she was going to get it.

I straightened and found my courage. "You've never done anything to help me. You've been lying to me and using me, and you've never once cared about how I felt."

She didn't deny it. She tipped her chin back and waited.

"You kidnapped me to use as blackmail to make my father work for you. When that didn't work, you sent me to Rott." The horrid memories of the burning factory and scalding acid rain washed over me, and my voice wobbled. "How was that 'for my own good'? I almost *died.*"

"You were supposed to," she whispered.

I froze and looked at her.

She dropped the med scanner back in her bag. "Philadelphia was supposed to die on Rott. You were supposed to have an untimely 'accident' so you could come back as Andromeda."

It all made sense—horrid, ugly sense. I let the bitterness and pain bleed into my voice. "Right, so you could 'adopt' me and take me from my father."

There was a pause—too long. "He never told you, did he?"

Ice rippled up my arms. "He who? Told me what?"

She shook her head. "Thames. He never told you about your father."

"What about my father?"

Oh God, not again.

To her credit, her eyes looked wistful and sad as she relayed, "Your father knew about the whole thing. He agreed to work on Red Rain in exchange for us giving you a new life."

My pounding heartbeat echoed in the concrete room like a bullet ricocheting off the walls.

"We didn't 'take' you, Andromeda," Mrs. Nolan said. "Your father gave you up."

9

"You're lying!" I screeched, and desperately needed it to be true.

But I knew that it wasn't. I remembered my father's indifference, his dry eyes, his cold willingness to let me get shipped away to Rott, and I recognized what I should have seen all along.

My father knew exactly what was going on. He knew what he had done—what he had done to me.

Just go.

"I have the paperwork," Mrs. Nolan said.

Tears raged down my face. "Well, thank God my paperwork now says something else." I'd never been more grateful that Nic had agreed to be Andromeda's guardian; anything to keep this woman from having legal power over me. I swiped at my eyes and ran for the door.

She let me go, but she called after me. "You can't keep running from this, Andromeda."

I threw the door open. *Yes, I can.*

"You can't keep running from me."

I hesitated in the doorway and glared back at her. She stood there, arms wide. "We're family now."

I slammed the door shut again. "So that's it? You want me to just say 'I forgive you,' and we walk out of here as mother and daughter?"

Her eyes glittered with tears. "I would love that."

My gut hurled. *You will never be my mother.*

She spoke before I could formulate words. "But I know it can't be that way."

She took a deep breath and sponged her eyes with the back of her hand. "Things weren't supposed to be this way. You were never supposed to go to Mars. You were supposed to come home, become Andromeda, and start over. My husband was going to wait until things calmed down and then give your father and brother new jobs. You were even going to be able to visit them." She blinked away the last of her tears and looked at me. "We never intended to keep you from your father. You must believe me when I say that."

I did believe her, and that scared me.

I should have listened to Mrs. Nolan and insisted you stay on Earth. None of this would have happened if you hadn't gone to Mars.

"But after you released the virus, Carnegie wanted to use you as a scapegoat—and as bait to find your father."

Her choice of words startled me. "So you *did* know exactly what you were doing," I accused, and waited for her to defend herself.

She didn't. "Yes, we did."

For the first time since we'd met, I felt validated and understood—and a tiny bit less afraid.

My heart rate began to slow even as my mind sped up. "But that doesn't make it any better. You—Thames—could have prevented all of this. He could have told Carnegie no."

"I know," she admitted, "and he should have. That's why I know things can never be the same between us."

She released her breath, and her whole body seemed to sag. "I know you suffered terrible things up there. You were mistreated, and you've had to fight for yourself and make horrible decisions no young woman should ever have to make— all because of what my husband did to you. As soon as they released that first video, I knew your life was ruined, and I'd never get to bring my Andromeda home."

Her tears returned, and they seemed genuine. I let her weep silently and struggled to decide how to think, how to feel.

"What do you want from me?" I whispered.

She looked up through her veil of tears, not bothering to wipe them away this time. "I want you to let me help you."

I shook my head. "You can't—"

She put up her hand. "No, it's your turn to listen. You don't know me, Andromeda. You don't know how I feel or why I did what I did. And while I don't expect you to understand, I need you to know that I did it because I genuinely wanted to help you."

Every muscle in my body tensed, but the Holy Spirit brushed by my ear with a warning.

Wait.

Mrs. Nolan coughed. Her voice came through clear and unashamed as she explained. "I know you see me as a predator, but when I first met you, what I saw was a poor young girl who was growing up in prison. I saw a girl who had to live in poverty and go to school at *gunpoint* because someone with power hated her religion."

The obvious implication hit me. "And you *don't* hate my religion?"

She glared at me. "Since when have I ever implied that I hate your religion?"

I scrolled back through our conversations and realized that the Nolans had never once tried to get me to deny Christ. They'd never even asked me to sign the file, at least not directly.

Come with me, Philadelphia, and you can keep your Bible in peace.

"But why?"

She regarded me with a lifetime of sadness. "Do I need a reason not to hate you?"

Everyone else does.

She spread her hands. "You won't believe me when I say it's because I love you, but I do. I knew your father wasn't coming back from Mars, and I knew that if you stayed behind, Ambrose would place you with a family whose sole job it was to bully you out of your identity. And if that failed and you aged out of the system, you'd get thrown back in prison to be tried as an adult. Do you know how that makes me feel as a mother?"

Her eyes wandered the shooting range as she measured her next words. "To me, it was no different than adopting any other orphan. I had the money and privilege to give you what others could not: a clean file. I believed—knew—that you'd be better off with me than on your own."

I might have accepted that explanation, if it weren't for one fatal flaw in her logic. "But I wasn't an orphan."

She didn't sugarcoat it. "You soon would have been."

"But you had the power to change that." My eyes burned with the pain of a reality she still refused to see. "Thames was controlling the whole thing. He could have saved my dad. He could have kept us together. The only reason I needed to be adopted was because of the things *he* did. How can you expect me to believe that's love?"

"I'm not asking you to."

I threw my hands out. "Then what are you asking?"

She met my eyes. "I'm asking you not to hate me."

I stared back.

Get rid of all bitterness, rage and anger...

She shook her head. "Andromeda, you're the one that's trying to reconcile your beliefs with mine. I'm not asking you to justify me. I'm not asking you to agree with me. I did what I thought was right, and you did what you thought was right, and I don't expect us to ever see eye to eye on it."

...brawling and slander, along with every form of malice....

"I hope we can be friends," she continued, her voice strained under the weight of regret, "but if we can't, I understand. But don't refuse medical help because you hate me. Don't walk around with a fractured rib just because you're mad at me."

Be kind and compassionate to one another...

She retrieved the scanner from her bag. She turned it on and extended her hand one more time. "Let me help you."

...forgiving each other, just as in Christ God forgave you.

I took a step towards her.

She didn't smile, but something flickered across the back of her eyes. "Let me see."

I gingerly lifted my shirt to reveal the bruise that was spreading across my side.

She toggled the settings on the scanner, then knelt next to me so she was eye-level with my wound. "Take a deep breath and hold it for ten seconds."

I obeyed. She panned the device slowly over my ribs, brow furrowed as she focused on the readouts.

"All right, you can let it out." She fiddled with the device for a minute, then put it back in her bag. She retrieved a wireless stethoscope and put on the earpiece. "Take three slow breaths for me."

I put my shirt back down and focused on taking deep, long breaths. She stood in front of me and moved the stethoscope around my chest. Then she stepped back and pulled the earpiece out.

"Well, you're right—it's not fractured, and your lungs sound good. But I want you to do some breathing exercises so you don't get in the habit of breathing shallowly. That will lead to even worse problems."

"Yes ma'am."

She took out her phone and started typing. "I'll send the instructions to your tablet—you can do it when you get home. Feel free to ice frequently, and you might try sleeping partially upright for the next few nights."

"Okay. Do you have any pain medication?"

That time, she smiled. "Yes, I do. I'll send some over when I get back to the infirmary."

"Thank you." I hesitated—feeling, wondering if there was more to say. "I'll bring your hoodie back tomorrow."

"What hoodie?" she said without looking up from her phone.

"The gray one you loaned me yesterday. I'm washing it."

She shrugged. "Wasn't mine."

Then whose is it?

I waited for a second more. When I realized neither of us was going to say anything else, I picked up my backpack and let myself out.

"Andromeda," she called as I stepped out into the hall, "no more shooting until I say so."

I glanced back. "Doctor's orders?"

She winked. "Doctor's orders."

I smiled, thanked her again, and left.

10

The shred of peace I'd managed to scrape together evaporated when I walked into the lab and saw Ephesus with his head in his hand, muttering.

He sat next to Dad. I glanced around the room; Stanyard was nowhere to be seen. I rapped my knuckles on the doorframe. "Ephesus?"

He broke off and looked up at me with bloodshot eyes. "Hey, sis. Sorry, just talking to Dad."

I wanted to ask him what he'd said, but somehow I felt that his grief was not mine to share. He was an innocent victim; none of this was his fault.

"Any luck with the memory dump?"

He gestured at an empty chair; I dragged it over and sat down next to him.

"No," he admitted. "This OS is completely foreign to me. And since it's a proprietary—and potentially lethal—device, Kaylon hasn't exactly been generous with publishing its code on the web." He paused. "But I'll keep trying," he added, more to himself than to me.

The last sentence held absolutely no hope at all, so I didn't bother to acknowledge it. "Did you try the passcodes Nic sent?"

He nodded. "All of them. No luck. Stanyard's program is trying a randomized password every five minutes."

I didn't need him to tell me how futile an effort that was. *What do we do now, Jesus?*

"Did you go see Mrs. Nolan?" Ephesus's voice was starched with cheerfulness.

"She found me, yeah," I said, and didn't elaborate, even after he questioned me with a raised eyebrow. "She says nothing's fractured and my lungs sound fine."

"Good." He sighed and leaned back in the chair, his eyes on Dad's.

I watched him. "Why are you and Mrs. Nolan…" I backpedaled when I realized how accusatory that question sounded. "How did you find her?"

"She was treating me while I was sitting in jail, waiting for Thames to decide what to do with me." He tapped the bandage on his nose. "She brought me info on Dad and Cea."

That matched what Cea had told me, but it didn't explain how Mrs. Nolan had been promoted from prison nurse to friend. "Why is she here?"

He turned to me. "She helped me escape. When you released that virus on Rott, it sent Thames's headquarters into a panic, and Mrs. Nolan helped me slip out. She hid me at one of their rental properties while we tried to figure out what happened with Dad and Cea—but they both dropped off the grid."

"Cea was looking for you." With a laugh that wasn't quite happy, I remembered the message I was supposed to pass along. "She wanted me to tell you that she loves you."

A smile slowly warmed his features. "What inflection did she put on that?"

"What inflection do you *want* me to put on that?" I said, eying him.

He dodged the question. "When did she leave for Mars?"

I fumed playfully at him, but the only response I got was a wink. With a grunt to express my displeasure, I answered, "Wednesday."

"She should land tomorrow or Sunday then—I'll call her."

Seeing I wasn't going to get any more romantic gossip out of him, I circled the conversation back around. "So you've been at the Nolans' apartment this whole time?"

He shook his head. "No, when the government busted Thames's office, we both dropped off the grid. I saw your livestream and knew Thames was dead, and she'd be next. So I convinced her to come with me, and we…"

He kept talking, but his words were lost in the torrent of emotion that rushed through me. Mrs. Nolan was a widow. I knew that, of course—I was there when it happened.

Ephesus touched my shoulder. "You did the right thing, turning Thames in," he said, as if reading my thoughts.

"I know." There was no room in my cluttered subconscious for guilt or regret over Thames's death. But I had never stopped to acknowledge that Mrs. Nolan had lost a loved one, too—and unlike my father, there was no hope that Thames could come back.

"Any luck?"

I started and looked behind me. Jayde stood in the doorway.

Ephesus straightened. "No. Kaylon's code is completely proprietary, and none of my backdoors work."

"Did you try the passcodes from Q?"

Ephesus shook his head. "Nothing."

Jayde grunted.

"Nic will send me more tomorrow," I offered. "He said he was going to search Carnegie's personal devices…"

I tripped over the word. Both boys looked at me. I grabbed Ephesus's arm. "Carnegie's phone."

He wasn't impressed. "Huh?"

"Carnegie—surely he had a phone on him when he died. Did you search the room when you went back for Dad? Can we still get into that building?" I swiveled to face Jayde.

He shrugged. "I can send some guys, but I'm sure his allies have razed the place—if the cops didn't get there first. But we can try searching his phone again."

"Again?" I asked, and suddenly realized I probably didn't want the answer.

He raised an eyebrow, as if my incompetence amused him. "We've got his body in the morgue."

*

There he was, lying on a slab, looking only slightly paler in death than he had in life.

I'm not sure why I wanted to see him. My subconscious did not need any more morbid images to warp into nightmares. Perhaps I just wanted to reassure myself that he was one figment of my past who wouldn't be coming back to haunt me.

I nodded at Jayde, who pulled the sheet back over Carnegie's face. Ephesus muttered something under his breath.

Stanyard and Lev had joined us in the morgue—although "morgue" was a luxurious term for what was clearly a storeroom that had been retrofitted with tables and a walk-in freezer. I didn't ask if the freezer had been repurposed, or if it had been specially installed for storing bodies.

"Why do you have him in here?" I asked.

Jayde wheeled the gurney towards the freezer. "I figured if we cleaned up the evidence, it would give his allies a bit of a chase."

"Although I'm sure they've figured out he's gone dark by now." Lev dragged the freezer door open; I deftly avoided looking inside.

"Here's his personal effects." Stanyard dropped a box on an empty exam table.

I walked over, Ephesus a step behind me, and scanned the contents. There wasn't much: a keyfob, an expensive pen that looked like it was more for show than for writing, and two phones.

"We've got his car out back." Stanyard picked up the keyfob. "But it's empty except for a carjack and some cold coffee."

I took the phones out of the box. One was shiny, slim, and new. The other was old, chunky, and scratched—not unlike the early 2000s touchscreens we used as burners.

I glanced at Jayde. "Can I turn them on?"

He nodded. "Yeah, I took both of them offline and disabled the passcodes."

Ephesus picked up the newer device and frowned at it. "How'd you do that? Wasn't this thing locked?"

Jayde arched his eyebrow, a gesture I was quickly learning to loathe. "It's not like I don't have Carnegie's thumbprint."

Stanyard pulled a face that perfectly represented the disgust that shivered through my stomach.

Ephesus powered the phone on. I picked up the older device and did the same.

Jayde leaned his knuckles on the table. "We searched them once already and didn't find anything—but at the time I didn't know we were looking for a passcode."

Ephesus rapidly swiped through menus on the newer device. The old phone was still stuck on the loading screen.

After a minute, Ephesus shook his head and handed the new phone to me. "He had all his apps set to auto-purge data every twenty-four hours. Taking the device offline seems to have stopped the last purge, but there's almost nothing there."

Stanyard drummed his fingers on his arm. "It's like he was expecting to get caught."

"Smart man," Lev muttered.

I clicked on the texting app and saw that Ephesus was right. There were only a handful of active conversations, all dated from Wednesday. None of the numbers were associated with named contacts, but the meaning of the messages was obvious.

WE'VE GOT THE BUILDING SURROUNDED

SHE JUST RADIOED FOR BACKUP. EXITING VIA BOYLSTON. HER FRIENDS ARE WAITING

LET THEM GET THERE FIRST. IF YOU HAVE A CLEAR SHOT, TAKE IT

I clenched my hand around the device.

CONFIRMED, HE'S MAKING THE DROP TONIGHT, BEFORE 21:00

ARE YOU IN PLACE?

WE ARE

My forehead grew clammy at the same time my cheeks grew hot.

You led me right to him.

MACHINE IS INSTALLED AND WARMING UP. WILL BE READY TO FREEZE IN THREE HOURS. WILL EMAIL THE INVOICE

WE'VE GOT HIM. HE'S OUT, BUT NOT FOR LONG

I SAID YOU DIDN'T HAVE TO BE GENTLE

I pinched my eyes shut to keep the tears from escaping. *Daddy, I'm so sorry.*

There was one more conversation. It was between Carnegie and a foreign area code.

WHEN SHOULD I EXPECT DELIVERY?

SHOULD BE READY BY 22:30

The recipient hadn't acknowledged the text. They didn't reply until after eleven o'clock—late enough that Carnegie was long dead.

Apparently, the recipient was aware of that fact.

YOU FOOL

I turned the screen off.

"I can hook it up to my computer, run some diagnostics," Stanyard offered.

"Please," I said, and handed the device to him. I picked up the older phone, which had finally decided to come to work.

"That's just a burner," Lev offered. "There's nothing on there."

I opened the most recent text and instantly knew whose phone it was.

THIRD FLOOR. HURRY

Dad.

A quick skim of the chat history showed that he had, in fact, confirmed an appointment with Andes. Then there was silence except for my frantic messages to him. Carnegie must have taken the phone from his unconscious body and sent me the address.

I sucked in my breath.

You should have stayed on Mars, sweetheart.

"What is it, Phil?" Ephesus said from over my shoulder.

I quickly closed the chat. "Nothing. It's just a burner, like he said."

Jayde's eyebrows went up again. Ephesus, thankfully, didn't notice. He turned to Stanyard and started rambling about the various programs they could run on Carnegie's phone.

I angled myself away from him and opened the app again.

I scrolled to the bottom. Unlike Carnegie, Dad hadn't wiped his message history—probably because most of his messages had gone unanswered. Most of the texts appeared to be cold calls, asking if the number still belonged to a friend or if he could claim a long-expired IOU.

THIS IS CATALYST. I'M WONDERING IF I CAN COLLECT THAT FAVOR

Most of the texts didn't receive a reply. Several numbers were undeliverable. Of the few who did answer, most of them quickly fizzled into dead ends.

IT'S GOOD TO HEAR FROM YOU, BUT I'M NOT IN BUSINESS ANYMORE

CAN YOU AT LEAST TELL ME IF THERE'S BEEN ANY UPDATES ON HER FILE?

SORRY MAN, I CAN'T HELP YOU

The text history did tell me one thing: Dad had a large network, even if most of it had gone cold. Where had he gotten all these numbers? He'd texted dozens of people, which meant he'd either had their numbers memorized or knew where to look them up. How did he know so many people? I couldn't recall him ever mentioning having allies, let alone friends. We'd always been alone in the world; Dad used to warn me that there was no one outside the containment camp walls we could rely on.

That was, apparently, another lie. He had known these people once—and some, it seemed, still knew him.

IS THIS STILL BART'S NUMBER?

I WAS WONDERING HOW LONG IT WOULD TAKE YOU TO CALL

I pondered the message, which Dad had never answered, as Jayde's words from yesterday came floating back to me.

Your dad isn't who he says he is.

I jumped to the most recent conversations—the ones that had gotten replies.

IT'S GOOD TO HAVE YOU BACK, CATALYST

I'M NOT BACK, I JUST NEED A FAVOR

BUT WE NEED YOU

I'M JUST TRYING TO FIND BLUE FIRE

WE NEED HER TOO

I gripped the phone. Dad hadn't acknowledged the message, but the stranger hadn't given up, sending several more texts in short succession.

IT'S TIME TO COME BACK

YOU NEVER SHOULD HAVE QUIT

WE CAN STILL DO THIS

He's done this before.

IT'S TIME FOR OPERATION BLUE FIRE TO RETURN

I dropped the phone. It clattered on the metal exam table, sound like gunfire in the silent room.

Ephesus and Stanyard stopped and turned around.

I looked up. Jayde was staring at me, waiting.

I grabbed the edge of the table. "What's Operation Blue Fire?"

He straightened and gestured at the door. "Come and see."

11

The command center was both dank and blinding at the same time.

The overhead lights were off, as if they were trying to hide in the dark, even though there were no windows in the cavernous place. The temperature was at least ten degrees colder than the hall as the air conditioning fought to keep the blinking wall of servers cool. The chill, combined with the incessant whir of electronics that thrummed like a plague of locusts, made the place seem claustrophobic, even though it took up the entire top floor of the building.

But despite the fact that the corners were enshrouded in shadow, the center of the room was drowning in irritating blue light from hundreds of backlit screens. Dozens of computer stations were scattered around the room, and a circular command module dominated the open floor. At hand-height was a ring of control panels and touchpads, its buttons and levers glittering like a diamond necklace. Above it hung a seamless jumbotron. Random inputs flickered across it constantly like an overactive heart monitor, adding to the anxious chaos.

"It's smaller on the outside," Stanyard muttered from behind me.

There were about twenty people, most in military fatigue, working around the room. Jayde stepped in ahead of us and clapped his hands. "Captain on the bridge!"

Everyone stopped and stood at attention, a fluid motion honed by discipline. The man standing nearest to us—an officer, judging by the number of pins and bars on his uniform—turned and spotted me.

"Blue Fire," he acknowledged, and saluted.

Around the room, everyone else followed suit.

I clenched my fists. "Don't call me that." I felt angry, but my voice just came out small and weak. Scared.

The officer turned to Jayde with a confused frown. Jayde jerked his thumb towards the door. "Clear the room."

They obeyed. Stanyard, Ephesus, and I stepped out of the way to let them pass. I felt all eyes on me as they walked by, even though I stubbornly avoided returning any of their stares.

As soon as the room was empty except for Lev, I turned to Jayde. "Can't you tell them not to call me that? We're not on the radio."

He shrugged. "It's who you are to them." He turned his back on me and walked over to the command module. He swiped on a touchpad, and a video I knew all too well started playing on the monitors: the security footage from Rott.

He gestured at the screen. "As soon as this video started trending, you became Blue Fire."

"I don't understand," I said, and frankly, I didn't want to.

"I was in the room with Thames when you and Q blew up the factory on Rott. I saw the livestream of the security footage at the same time he did—and managed to rip it before he classified it." He looked at me and waited to see if I understood the implications.

I did. "You're the one who leaked the video."

He nodded. "Stanyard and I uploaded it to our social media."

I glanced back at Stanyard. He did not avoid my gaze. "We—I—thought you were dead. I wanted the world to know why."

I studied him, trying to gauge his emotions, but Jayde wasn't interested in letting us have a moment. "We weren't the only ones. We spammed our contacts, and they repeated the process. You were an instant phenomenon."

I knew that; I'd seen the views on some of my videos. What I didn't know was that my fame had been manufactured by the underground.

Ephesus was tracking the same thoughts. "Surely Thames helped promote her," he argued.

Jayde shrugged. "Maybe, but we could have done it without him. Everyone loved you." He turned to me again. "I had contacts I hadn't heard from in years asking me how they could help. That's when I knew you were the new Blue Fire."

Stanyard made a noise that could best be described as a growl. "You told me you made up that callsign—"

I put up a hand to stop him. "'New' Blue Fire?" I repeated, my eyes on Jayde.

He didn't make me wait. "Your father was the first."

I wanted to deny it. I wanted to scream that he was lying and slam the door in his face, just like I'd done with Mrs. Nolan, and Thames, and Carnegie, and everyone else who had come before him. They had all lied to me. Everyone had—including Daddy.

But somehow I knew that Jayde wasn't. For the first time in my life, someone was telling me the honest truth, and it was terrifying.

"Dad?" Ephesus breathed.

Jayde toggled more menus, and Dad's file appeared on the screen. "Your father has been transmitting Bibles since high school. He and several others built a network of people willing to share censored media across the globe. They called it Operation Blue Fire."

That wasn't entirely news to me, although I'd never heard it spelled out in so many words. I knew Dad was a transmitter, and always had been, but I thought he only did it for friends and local contacts through his job. He had done more when he was younger, but that was before I was born—before Grandpa Andrew had gotten convicted for transmitting.

I had no idea he'd built an international network around it.

It's good to have you back, Catalyst.

"Anyone who knew the symbol could get a download." Jayde scrolled down, but I knew what I was going to see before the image even loaded: that haunting bird with a lightning bolt in its claws.

"A thunderbird," Lev answered my unspoken question.

There it was, on my father's file, the same image that Cea and Andes had. Were they both part of the same transmitting network? Had they worked with my father? Surely Cea would have mentioned it if she knew my father was involved.

I glanced at Ephesus to see if the image meant anything to him, but he was squinting at the screen, looking as pale and lost as I felt. Clearly, Dad had lied to both of us.

I shoved the queasy emotion aside. "But what does this have to do with me and my videos?" I'd transmitted a few Bibles in my lifetime, but it certainly wasn't what I was known for.

"Your father wasn't just transmitting any Bibles." Jayde clicked a button and entered a passcode, and my father's file, which was already long and peppered with warnings, doubled in length and lit up like a firework. "After you were taken into camp, they developed a plan to use censored media to spread coded information. The Bibles would be edited to include hidden messages and then distributed on the network. The theory was that if the government found illegal Bibles, they'd just delete them, never realizing they contained classified plans."

"Clever," Ephesus murmured, and he sounded sincere. I couldn't decide if that idea was sacrilegious or brilliant. It was at least a little more practical than scorching Earth with chemical warfare.

I took a deep breath and braced myself for the drop. "And what exactly were these plans for?"

Lev was the first to answer. "Revolution," he said, his Russian accent slurring the word into something thick and sinister.

Ephesus went completely still, as if he'd died standing up. Stanyard sucked his breath in sharply through his nose. All eyes turned to me and waited, as if expecting me to have a reaction.

I didn't know what to say.

Lev walked over to the other side of the control module and started typing. A map of the East Coast engulfed the screen, the topography muddied by dozens of crosses, lines, and coordinates written in bloodred. "The unassimilated camps made everyone angry—they were ready to act. So we came up with a plan to liberate the camps and end them for good."

Ephesus and I shared an involuntary look. *End the camps?* I'd never dreamed that was possible. I couldn't even imagine a world without religious persecution, a world where my identity wasn't illegal and shunned.

Could freedom like that be possible?

Stanyard jumped to the obvious conclusion. "What went wrong?"

"Catalyst dropped out," Jayde said, the bitterness unveiled in his voice. For a brief moment, the light went out of his eyes as he turned his glare on me.

You never should have quit.

I held his stare. "Why?"

Compassion rushed back into his expression as he whispered, "Your mother."

My face and hands grew numb as everything snapped into place. The lies, the blood splatter in the entryway, the police report on my father's file. All the deception to cover up the real reason my mother had died.

Ephesus moaned. "Oh, Mom..."

Jayde tapped the screen, and a crackly audio recording started playing. I walked up next to him to listen, even though I couldn't remember willing my feet to move.

There was a shower of static, and then the recording began in the middle of someone's sentence.

"—happened? I saw the call go out for an ambulance to your area, but no one could tell me anything. I was so—"

The person abruptly silenced. My mind strained at the voice; I'd heard it before, somewhere. "Do you recognize him?" I asked Ephesus.

His face was pinched in confused agony. "I—I'm not sure."

My dad was the next to speak, the heartbreak obscuring his words more than static ever could. *"Blue Fire is down."*

"Mom," Ephesus whispered.

I glanced at him.

"It was Mom's childhood nickname," he whispered, as if he were afraid to admit that it was true.

"Your father named the operation after her," Jayde echoed. "In honor of the Bibles she transmitted in high school."

The room swam as tears flooded my eyes. I pinched them shut and listened.

The other caller continued sputtering. *"Down? What do you mean? What happened? Is she okay? What hospital did they take her to? I'll see if I can—"*

"Tower! She's dead," my dad yelled, and my world stopped.

My eyes flew open. "Dad knew Tower?"

Jayde paused the recording. "They were in charge of the whole thing."

Stanyard stepped up beside me. "How do you know him?"

"He was a guard on Rott. He helped us destroy the factory." I replayed all our interactions in my mind and tried to sift out any signs of familiarity. He had been kind, of course, and willing to help, but he hadn't acted like he knew me. Did he not realize who I was, who my father was?

Lev and Jayde shared a glance, then Jayde hit play.

My father's voice came in again. *"They knew we were planning something. They came for the drive."*

I remembered the incident report on my father's file.

Police had been dispatched with a warrant to arrest Dr. Thomas Smyrna for the charges of transmitting illegal media...

Suddenly, Jayde's voice joined the recording. *"What did you do with it?"*

"I crushed it, just like I was supposed to," my father snapped, rage replacing the grief in his voice. *"And in the process my wife got shot."*

I slapped a hand over my mouth. Ephesus muttered an oath.

Dr. Smyrna resisted arrest. Officers drew weapons in an attempt to subdue him, and Abigail Smyrna was unintentionally shot...

Jayde had apparently wasted no time on grief that day. His recording was quick to demand, *"Yeah, and the rest of us would have too if you—"*

"Green Dragon, get off the line!" a stranger mercifully silenced him. I turned to Jayde. He was staring at the screen, face expressionless.

Tower continued. *"Catalyst, we need to get you out of there. I can arrange a pickup, tonight, 1900."*

"Belay that, Tower," Dad snapped. *"I'm fine. They can't prove anything. Don't come for me. Stay out of this."*

Tower was undeterred. *"No, I'm serious, I'm coming to get you. I'm tired of playing this game from the other side of the wall. I'm taking you both to safety, and then you're done."*

My heart skipped a beat. "You both" could have only meant Dad and me; Ephesus had been away at college at the time. Tower had been willing to come save us.

Dad's response was quick and panicked. *"Tower, no! Don't come for us, and don't try anything. That's an order."*

"Don't boss me around, old man. I—"

"Don't you get it?" Dad's shriek cracked the line. *"They know what we're doing. They're probably listening right now. If I try anything, my daughter goes into the system."*

I gasped. All eyes were on me again.

Ephesus touched my shoulder.

Tower's response was crushed with remorse. *"She's already in the system."*

"Yeah, well at least she's alive," Dad hissed.

I felt sick as the weight of the world dropped to my stomach.

Stay here. We're waiting for the officers to arrive.

"Catalyst, please," Tower begged. *"I promise I can do this safely. Let me come get you."*

"No," Dad snapped in a tone I knew all too well. *"Operation Blue Fire is over. We're not going anywhere."*

I'm not letting either of you get hurt anymore.

Jayde switched off the recording. I closed my eyes and willed the room—and everyone in it—to vanish.

Daddy, why did you lie to me?

Ephesus kneaded my shoulder, but his fingers felt cold and clammy. Stanyard was the first to speak. "Phil," he breathed. "I'm so sorry."

I drew an ugly sniff and tried to dam the tears back where they came from. I turned to Jayde. "What do you want with me?"

He spread his hands. "We need you to be the new Blue Fire."

I groaned. "What does that even mean? I still don't understand what any of this has to do with me," I said, even though it very clearly had *everything* to do with me. My father started all this—but that was in the past. That was before Mama died.

Now, I just wanted this conversation to be over.

"Why her?" Ephesus demanded, but not skeptically.

"Your videos made people angry," Jayde explained, all his focus still on me. "They're paying attention again. They'll act—if we give them a reason to. And you're that reason."

Only because you manufactured me into an idol.

"Operation Blue Fire is ready to launch," Lev echoed. "And you need to take your father's place."

I didn't appreciate his choice of words or the tone he used to say them. "Well, then you've got the wrong girl," I snapped. If they wanted a leader, they should have picked Ephesus. He'd done this before; he knew people in the underground.

I didn't know anything. I didn't belong here. I should be on Mars, keeping my head down, just like Nic told me to.

I brushed at the tears on my cheeks, even though more quickly fell to replace them. "I'm not my father. I don't know how to transmit, not like that. I don't have any contacts."

"You don't need them," Jayde said. "You're enough."

He put my video back on the screen and let it play. "People respect you, Blue Fire—they understand you. You're not some fancy hot shot with privilege and power who can buy your way out of trouble. At least Philadelphia isn't. She's a normal girl from the bottom of the food chain. An unassimilated. A nobody. A nobody who should be *dead.*"

He fast-forwarded to the part of the recording where the platform snapped, flinging me out of frame to my apparent demise.

"But you're not." He switched to another recording, the one I had strictly avoided rewatching.

"Their contact is a government agent named Thames. He has an office somewhere in the Boston metropolitan area..."

I pinched my eyes shut, knowing what was coming. Stanyard moved beside me. "Jayde..."

Jayde kept his hand on the button and left the video rolling. "You got up and kicked back. You had everything to lose, but you put yourself on the line to stop Thames and Carnegie—just like you fought Ambrose and Nic before them."

"He's right," Ephesus murmured, as if he'd never seen it before. His voice sounded far away, like he was also a video from my past.

Maybe he was. He didn't know me anymore. He didn't know who I'd become.

"It's not like that," I argued, but no one was listening to me. My own voice drowned me out as the video continued to play.

"You ruined yourself."

I slapped my hands over my ears.

"You don't understand. I could have helped you!"

"That's what people need to see," Jayde continued, raising his voice to be heard. "They need someone to show them that it can be done, to prove that there's something worth fighting for."

My scream ripped through the recording. There was a crack as I dropped the tablet, and the recording went dark. But the sound kept playing.

"We would have loved you!"

"Jayde, stop." Stanyard lurched forward and punched the control panel, shutting off the recording. But the damage was done. My memories supplied the gunshot, the screams, the blood.

Jayde took a step towards me. I jerked back. "Leave me alone!"

"I can't," he admitted. "I need you."

I stumbled into Ephesus, who braced me. "Phil, just listen to him. Maybe—maybe he's right."

I gaped up at him. *Are you on his side?*

Jayde came closer. "People won't follow me; they don't know me. But they know you."

"Then fine! Use my recordings. I don't care," I snarled, even though I definitely did. I just wanted to run. I just wanted to run and never see him or this place again. I slipped out of Ephesus's grasp.

"We need new recordings," Lev said. "We need you to get on air and rally everyone to the cause."

Horror rippled through me. "I can't go on air! Look at me!" I yanked on my short, ashen-blonde hair. "If the government finds out about Andromeda, I'm dead. Nic's dead."

Jayde grimaced. "Who cares about Nic?"

"I do!" I screeched, and realized it was true. "Don't you get it? I'm responsible for him—for everyone. It's my fault my dad's down there, frozen in a block of ice." I pointed and slammed the floor with my foot. "I did that. It's my fault he's almost dead, because I didn't listen to Nic and lay low."

"That's not your fault, Phil," Ephesus argued.

"Yes, it is," I declared, and for once, it wasn't guilt that ripped through me. It was rage.

Ephesus was wrong; they were all wrong. About Dad, about Blue Fire, about me. My dad wasn't a hero. He was a liar. He'd lied and put our entire family at risk, and now my mom was dead.

I wouldn't make the same mistake.

"But they'll follow you!" Jayde pleaded. "Look, I promise I know what I'm doing—"

He had the audacity to reach for my hand. I slapped him away. "No! I won't do it. As soon as Dad's thawed, we're going back to Mars. If you need a revolutionary, you're going to have to find someone else."

I turned and ran for the door, praying none of them would follow.

"Philadelphia," Jayde called, tone changing. He took a breath. "Please."

I gripped the door handle. "My name is Andromeda," I snapped without looking back. "And I am not your Blue Fire."

12

"Thanks for getting me home on time," I said as Stanyard pulled up to the curb in front of the Vons'. According to his dashboard clock, it was 4:52.

"Don't tell her I ran that last yellow light," he snarked as he put the car in park.

I acknowledged his weak attempt at humor with a half-smile, but the gesture felt like rolling a boulder uphill.

"Here." He fished something out of his pocket. "I think you should have this."

He laid it in my lap: Carnegie's phone.

"I pulled a memory dump and have the computer running some decryption programs on it, but…"

"But you don't think you'll find anything," I finished for him. I flipped the device over in my hand.

He didn't answer. He didn't need to. I unzipped my backpack and slid the phone into a pocket next to Dad's burner.

"Did you…" Stanyard drummed his fingers on the wheel and tried again. "Did you and Ephesus… talk?"

It was my turn to shrug. "Not really."

It was an exaggeration—Ephesus and I hadn't talked about anything. As soon as I'd run from the command room, I'd stumbled around until I found a bathroom. I'd locked the door, hid in the corner, and sobbed until I was too tired to feel panicked anymore. Then I'd washed my face and used the concealer I had in my backpack to cover up any signs of emotion.

I'd gone back to the lab, where Ephesus found me soon after.

"Did you know?" I demanded as soon as he walked in the door. I knew the answer, but I had to hear it from him. I had to know at least one family member hadn't lied to me about Mom's death.

"No," he said, his pain equal to mine. "Dad told me the same story as you."

"Do you think Mom knew?"

His answer was longer in coming. "No."

"He killed her," I said, even though the words scraped like knives on my throat. "It's his fault she's dead."

Someone had to say it.

Ephesus sighed. "Phil, I—"

"I'm not doing it," I cut him off. I could feel him staring at me, but I refused to look up.

"Is it because of Nic?"

"Yes," I said, even though that was only half the answer.

The real reason was I didn't want to be like my dad.

Ephesus took a breath like he was going to say something more, then wisely decided not to. He sat down at the computer and went back to his programming, typing one-handedly with agonizing slowness. We didn't speak again until it was time for me to leave. I spent the rest of the afternoon sitting with my knees to my chest, staring at Dad's body and silently begging him to explain to me why he hadn't told me the truth.

"Phil." Stanyard drew me back to the present with a sigh, the gesture more sound than name. "You know you don't have to, right?"

I turned to him. "What?"

He met my eyes. "Jayde. You can tell him no."

"I thought I just did."

"Do it again if you have to. You don't have to do this."

I searched his face. "Do you think I shouldn't?"

"I don't know." His answer was quick—prepared.

I waited. When he didn't elaborate, I decided to push the question I'd been harboring all afternoon. "Did you know? About Blue Fire. About… my dad."

He shook his head. "Jayde didn't tell me anything until today. I knew about the hashtag, but I thought he made it up. I didn't expect your videos to blow up like they did." His eyes wandered as he traced the dust on the dash with his finger. "And I don't think Jayde did either."

"You don't?"

"No. I don't think he expected it to work. I think he threw the hashtag on there to see if anyone would answer—and they did." He looked up at me again, eyes filled with admiration that bordered on fear. "He underestimated you, Phil. We all did."

A sharp rap on the window scared me out of my wits—and the need to reply. I turned to see Mrs. Von leering on the sidewalk, nose nearly smudging the glass.

I cringed and rolled down the window.

"You're late," she declared.

I glanced at the clock. *5:01.*

Stanyard leaned over. "I'm sorry, Mrs. Von Nieuwenhuyse, it's my fault."

"Uh huh." She straightened and started walking back towards the house. "Well, come on, you two. It's time to set the table."

"You… two?" I repeated.

She was already on the porch. "I'm not sending him home hungry. I'm no swine." The screen door slammed behind her.

Stanyard turned to me with a raised eyebrow.

I opened the door. "You'd better come in. If you don't, it'll throw off their groove, and they'll be unmanageable all evening."

He laughed and unbuckled his seat belt.

I'm not sure what Mrs. Von thought was going on, but whatever it was, she pulled out all the stops for it. The recipe she had been preparing was deemed unsatisfactory; she literally dumped the half-cooked food in the trash and switched to a fancy shrimp pasta instead. Mr. Von was delighted to have another man in the house and kidnapped Stanyard as soon as he walked in the door. He showed him the garage, and the basement, and the backyard, and then the garage again, because of course he forgot where he'd already been. Stanyard got three full tours of the house before dinner was done.

It was nice to have another body around the table, but I couldn't get a word in edgewise as the Vons spent the entire meal drilling Stanyard with questions. He fudged the answers to some of them—especially the inquiries about his own parents—but everything he said seemed to delight them. The leftovers had long since grown cold before they let us up from the table.

Stanyard tried to make a break for it, but they wouldn't have it. Mrs. Von shooed us both out of the kitchen, claiming it was "her turn to clean up." Before Stanyard could even make a move towards the front door, Mr. Von grabbed him by the shoulders and steered him towards the living room. No sooner had Mr. Von queued up a movie than his wife appeared with bowls of ice cream. She handed one to each of us, winked at me, and waltzed back out of the room.

Stanyard stared at his mound of whipped cream and chocolate syrup. "Are they like this every night?"

I stabbed mine with my spoon. "No, they never bring out the ice cream for me."

He chuckled. "You've been spending too much time with Nic."

My brain restarted when I remembered that I was supposed to call him. I picked up my tablet, which I'd set on the coffee table, and was unsurprised to find a new message from him.

I TOLD YOU TO CALL ME WITH AN UPDATE

I was too tired to be anything but truthful.

I FORGOT

He immediately came online and responded.

WELL, LET ME JOG YOUR MEMORY

I let the silence hang for a minute while I figured out how to respond. I didn't want to talk. The last thing I wanted to do was rehash the trauma all over again and suffer through Nic's biting commentary on my trainwreck of a family.

Nic waited patiently for me to fulfill my duty. I was somewhat surprised that he didn't initiate a call just to establish dominance.

I finally settled on a half-honest answer.

I'M EXHAUSTED. THERE'S NOTHING TO REPORT

Nothing except my dad is apparently a revolutionary who tried to overthrow the government, and that's why my mom is dead, and now they want me to finish the job.

Nic would want to know. He'd have to know eventually. But I didn't want to talk about it, not now. Not when I couldn't even talk about it with my own brother.

Nic, unfortunately, was feeling social.

I TAKE IT NONE OF THE CODES WORKED

NO

I'LL SEND MORE IN THE MORNING

THANKS

I tabbed away, but no sooner had I opened another window than more messages came through.

HOW'S YOUR RIB?

I begrudgingly switched back to the chat and responded.

I GOT IT TREATED

HOW ARE YOU FEELING?

That question could have meant several things depending on the inflection, but none of the plausible answers were information I wanted to divulge. I wasn't about to give him a detailed breakdown of my physical *or* emotional state.

I JUST NEED SLEEP

He didn't respond, but I could see he was still online, waiting.

I took the initiative and closed the chat.

Stanyard excused himself as soon as the credits rolled. I caught him in the entryway.

"Do you know whose hoodie this is?" I asked, holding it out. "Mrs. Nolan says it's not hers."

"Oh, it's mine."

I gripped the fabric and tried to decide how that made me feel.

He shrugged. "It was the only clean shirt I could find. You can keep it if you want."

I did want; it was the comfiest piece of clothing I'd ever worn. "But… why?"

He scrunched his nose. "Why not?"

There was no good answer to that, but I hung my mouth open like I had one.

He chuckled. "If you don't want it, I'll take it back. But if you like it, keep it. It's that simple."

Is it that simple?

The Holy Spirit laughed in my ear.

Yes, it is.

"Okay," I said, folding it over my arm. "Thank you."

He grinned.

My heart skipped a beat when I realized this was the second gift he'd given me in the last twenty-four hours. Since when had

Stanyard been so generous? The only thing he'd given me when we were growing up was a hard time.

Stanyard seemed to have no such reservations about the whole ordeal. Without another word, he turned and went to open the door, then stopped.

"It's unlocked," I said after the silence had gotten awkward.

He spun back around. "Do you want to go to church with me tomorrow?"

He blurted it so fast that it took me a minute to translate, and then a minute longer to realize it had been years since I'd heard the word.

"Church...?" I repeated.

He nodded. "Yeah, I heard of one that's meeting across town tomorrow."

I ran the math and remembered what day it was. "Are we Seventh-day Adventists now?"

He shrugged. "You take what you can get in the apocalypse."

"I guess so." I struggled to wrap my mind around what he was proposing. "I just... didn't realize there were any churches left."

I tried to remember the last time I'd been in anything that resembled a church service. Public religious gatherings had been branded as seditious long before I was born. We'd tried to skirt the law, of course; I remembered meeting in basements, abandoned warehouses, old barns—even sketchy motel rooms in parts of town I probably shouldn't have been in—all to gather with the few friends we had left.

We'd gotten caught several times. Twice we managed to escape. The next time, only a few of us were left behind—not enough to prove that there had been a "gathering." They'd fined the adults and slapped felonies on everyone's files, including mine.

The final time—the last service I could remember attending—they surrounded the building and arrested everyone. Stanyard's family had been there too. My father and Mr. Dass spent over a week in prison, and for several days my mother feared they wouldn't be released.

They finally were, and my mother begged Daddy not to attend any more services. I don't remember what he said, but I clearly remembered what Stanyard said to me the next day at school.

"I'm never going to church ever again. It's not worth it."

Was it worth it now?

I searched his face. "Is it safe?"

"No less so than being on base."

He had a point there.

"I invited Ephesus. If it helps."

It did. "When do we need to leave?"

He smiled. "I'll come get you at 8 am."

13

It was unlike any church service I'd ever been in.

They were meeting underneath an abandoned parking garage, in a service tunnel that had once connected to the subway. It was accessible only by the stairwell, where they posted guards who looked suspiciously like subway maintenance crew. Stanyard showed them a text on his phone—proving that he'd talked to someone who knew someone—and they flagged us in.

The twang of an electric guitar floated up to us as we descended the last flight of greasy stairs. When we reached the landing, another guard used a handheld device to scan us for electronics and weapons. I wasn't surprised to find that Stanyard was carrying, but I was surprised when he surrendered his pistol without complaint.

Ephesus was less joyful about turning over his devices, of which he had a physically improbable number stuffed in his coat pockets. I only had Carnegie's phone and Dad's burner on me, but they still forced me to add them to the pile.

Satisfied we were clean, the guard ushered us through the door. We stepped into the tunnel, and I was instantly assaulted with the moan of collective prayer. A decent group of people—at least forty or fifty—had already gathered. The tunnel was wide enough for two trucks to pass, but the shape of the room still made the crowd look like a disorderly line. They clustered around the far end of the room, where the tunnel ended in a brick wall.

The floor sloped downward as the tunnel descended, allowing us to see all the way to the front. A crude stage had been erected from palettes and plywood, on top of which played an even cruder band. The drum kit was an eccentric combination of actual drums and vaguely acoustic buckets, and the electric guitar was hooked up to an old car battery. The band members, all two of them, warmed up with a wordless tune while a black man paced the stage, evidently leading the crowd in prayer.

"Lord, You said when two or three are gathered, You're going to show up. So I declare protection over this building, protection over the people who risked their lives and their freedom and their jobs to come here…"

More people shoved their way through the door. I watched the melting pot of skin color and affluence flow past and wondered where all these people had come from. Why weren't they in containment camps? Had they all signed the file?

Stanyard interrupted my thoughts. "Is that a fog machine?" He pointed to the corner of the stage.

It sure was, although it looked like it was made out of more duct tape than plastic. It intermittently hacked smog over the crowd, adding to the visual chaos.

"More like a smoke machine," Ephesus commented, and coughed.

"Don't insult Penelope! She's been through a war!"

I jumped when someone spoke from behind me—then breathed a prayer when I recognized the voice.

"Two wars, in fact," his partner said.

"Wait, what was the second one? Have you been to a war I don't know about?"

I turned around. "John? Dowe?"

They immediately went into battle mode, putting their hands up like a pair of clumsy superheroes. "Hey! How'd you know our code names?" one of them—God knows which one—said.

"Wait. Those are our code names?" The other lowered his arms and stared at his partner. "I thought those were our real names."

"I honestly can't remember," the first said without missing a beat.

"John," I said slowly, and watched to see which one reacted. "Dowe. It's me."

They sized me up with a squint, just like they had when we first met on Rott, and rightfully so. After some deliberation, I'd decided to go as Andromeda, piercings and all. If we were caught, it would be better for Andromeda to be fined for attending an illegal service than for Philadelphia to hang for her family's crimes.

It took a second—a long, painful second—but I was eventually rewarded with identical grins.

"Philadelphia!" they boomed together, and then rushed me in a hug. They both squished me at once, and while my soul appreciated the affection, my bruised rib did not.

"Ow, rib, ow," I complained, loud enough to be heard over their gushing.

"Sorry, sorry," Dowe said, and they freed me. "We're just so happy to see you. You know you've died, like, three times in the past month, right?"

"I think she's up to four," John argued. "There's Rott, and then that stunt on the TV, and then—"

"Don't mind if I ask, but..." Ephesus shoved himself physically and verbally into the conversation. "Do you know these guys?"

John sniffed at him, as if he could judge him by his smell. "The question is, do *you* know these guys? Because you should. We're awesome."

"You're something all right," Stanyard muttered.

Both John and Dowe turned on him in choreographed unison. "Well, what do you know," Dowe remarked. "She's brought another guy home."

"I swear she has a new one every time we meet her," John agreed.

Ephesus raised his eyebrow, Stanyard turned red and white at the same time, and I blanched. "I'm not 'bringing him home'!"

They weren't listening. "At least he's more her age than Q was."

"Yeah, but Q has a *base*."

"Fair, fair. She should really reconsider."

Stanyard shook his head to rattle his composure back into place. "Will someone please tell me what's going on?"

I took control of the conversation. "This is John and Dowe. I met them on Rott. They're friends." I looked to them, giving them a chance to prove me wrong.

John smiled. "The originals."

"But how did you get here?" I asked, reality catching up with me—although reality was always a slippery concept with John and Dowe. "What happened to Rott?"

John shrugged. "The cops told us we didn't have to go home, but we couldn't stay there."

"What he means to say is, we found out our sentence was up... *six years ago.* We could have gone home any time, but *someone* forgot to tell me." Dowe thwacked John in the back of the head.

"You're kidding, right?" Ephesus said.

I shook my head. "They never are."

Stanyard scratched the back of his neck. "I may have picked the wrong church..."

"Nonsense! This is the finest congregation this side of the Charles. Just wait until you meet our pastor." John turned and started screaming into the crowd.

"Never mind it's the only church this side of the Charles," Dowe muttered with a wink at me.

Ephesus turned to Stanyard. "Are you sure this place is safe? It's awfully... *loud* for something that's supposed to be off the radar."

"If you wanted quiet, you should have gone back to your concentration camp."

We turned to see a tall black man emerge from the crowd. I recognized him as the man who had been on the stage a moment before. He was built slim but powerful, his button-up tightly cuffed over his muscular arms. His head was shaved and his beard trimmed to perfection, and a gold chain glinted around his neck. He didn't look anything like what I had imagined the pastor of an underground church to be, but he did look like he meant business.

Ephesus sized him up. "What did you say?"

"If you wanted quiet, you should have gone back to your concentration camp," the man repeated, not unkindly. "We don't do quiet here."

Ephesus shifted but did not back down. "Aren't you afraid of getting busted?"

The man shrugged. "If Daniel was afraid of getting caught, he would have closed the window. Name's DeMarcus." He went to offer Ephesus a handshake, then settled for a pat on the shoulder instead.

Ephesus studied him for a beat more, then smiled. "Klez. Are you the pastor here?"

"Something like that," Pastor DeMarcus said with a twinkle. "I just bring the preaching. These saints organize the meeting." He gestured at John and Dowe.

"You... organized this?" I said, and wondered if I'd underestimated them all along.

They bowed with a flourish. "That's us—John and Dowe, your friendly neighborhood event coordinators! We have over thirty years of experience. Worship services, coups, weddings, distractions—you name it, we can plan it!"

I grinned. I knew from experience that they did, in fact, know how to plan a good distraction.

Pastor DeMarcus extended his hand to Stanyard. "And you must be Augustine. They told me you'd be bringing friends."

Stanyard accepted the handshake, and Pastor DeMarcus pulled him into a manly slap on the back. Then he turned to me. "And you are?"

"Andromeda." It felt weird to be the only one not using a callsign, but I wasn't about to admit that I was Blue Fire.

"Ooh, pretty," John or Dowe crowed.

Pastor DeMarcus held out both his hands. I stretched mine forward—and winced when the gesture pulled on my rib.

Pastor DeMarcus frowned.

"Just a bruise," I fudged.

"Could we pray for you?" Then, without waiting for an answer, he turned and gestured at someone across the room.

"I mean, sure," I fumbled. I couldn't remember the last time someone, let alone a complete stranger, had asked to pray for me.

A beautiful woman came to stand beside the pastor. Her skin was caught somewhere between black and white, and her raven-dark hair fell over her shoulders in heavy curls.

"This is my wife," Pastor DeMarcus said by way of introduction. He bent and whispered something in her ear.

She stepped towards me, hazel eyes searching me softly. "Is it okay if I put my hand on your rib?"

"I mean, sure," I said again, not sure what else to say.

She did, laying her warm fingers gently on my wound. She raised her other hand in the air as she started praying in tongues, her face set in concentration. Pastor DeMarcus followed suit, putting both arms up.

I just watched. I didn't know what to do except let it happen.

Abruptly, she switched to English. "Jesus, you are our healer. Come and heal this daughter of yours. Pain *goes*. Swelling *goes*. Strength returns."

Ephesus came up behind me and put his hand on my shoulder. Stanyard tentatively raised one hand halfway.

Across the room, the band kicked in. Someone jumped up on the stage and shouted a welcome that was answered with a rousing *Amen*. The guitarist began to sing a chorus, and the rest of the crowd joined him. Soon the entire room was clapping in beat, the sound echoing around the concrete structure and multiplying like rain turning into a storm.

Our God is an awesome God, He reigns from heaven above...

The woman took her hand away. "How do you feel?"

Dizzy, would have been the appropriate response. The music was thunderous in the narrow tunnel, and I felt warm all over. I took a deep breath, hoping for a miracle—but it still hurt to breathe. What was I supposed to expect?

"I don't know," I finally answered.

She smiled. "Give it time. It's good to have you all with us." She acknowledged everyone with a nod, then squeezed her husband's arm and blended back into the crowd.

Pastor DeMarcus turned to follow. "Let's worship."

We watched him walk away. The stragglers around the room were all flowing towards the stage, leaving our group alone on the outskirts.

"Let's go!" John and Dowe encouraged. "You can stand with us."

One of them took my arm. I allowed them to pull me towards the crowd. Ephesus and Stanyard mercifully stayed close behind.

We joined the edge of the throng. There was no cohesiveness to the crowd at all; everyone seemed to have their own idea of what worship meant. Some had their hands to the sky; others, their face to the floor. Some danced with as much passion as you would at a club; others were so still I might have thought them dead. Everyone sang at different volumes. Some weren't singing in English at all.

What am I supposed to do?

Dowe playfully jostled me. "Sing with me! This is my favorite song."

"But I don't know the words," I panicked.

I saw the Lord, seated on His throne... He was clothed in glory, and exalted high...

"Then make up your own!" John chirped, and started doing just that. He put his hands up and started babbling about how good God had been to him, in a key that didn't match the band at all. Dowe was doing the same, although he was closer to being in tune.

Ephesus watched them for a moment. Slowly, he lifted one hand. "God, thank you for saving me." He made no attempt to sing, but his voice grew louder as he recited his blessings—just like he would if he were praying at the kitchen table. "I should be dead, but you rescued me. Thank you for protecting me, and my sister..."

Something nipped at my cheeks and my ears and neck began to burn.

I opened my mouth, but I couldn't think of anything to say. I had a million things to be thankful for—didn't I?—but none of the words would form. I normally didn't have a problem talking to Jesus. Why couldn't I now? Was it the music? Was it the crowd? Was it too loud in here? No one else seemed to have any issues praying or singing. Was I doing something wrong?

His name is Jesus... His name is Wonderful, Counselor, Almighty God...

Pastor DeMarcus climbed on the stage. Abruptly, the singing tapered off, lowering the ambiance. He didn't have a microphone, but he didn't need one as his powerful voice boomed over the crowd.

"If anyone needs prayer, if anyone needs healing, the front is open. Don't let this moment pass you by! Don't leave here the same person you came in."

"Don't have to tell me twice!" John cheered. "Hey Klez, wanna come?" He grabbed Ephesus's good arm.

"I, uh—" Ephesus stammered.

He needn't have bothered; neither of them was listening. Dowe slapped his shoulder. "Don't worry, we'll go with you! Come on, Andromeda."

"I already got prayer," I blurted without even thinking.

John shrugged. "They don't charge for refills." Without waiting for my response, they dragged Ephesus into the crowd and disappeared. I was left with Stanyard on my side and a frantic throng pressed all around me, screaming the words to a song I didn't know.

How great is our God, sing with me, how great is our God...

This couldn't be right. There was so much noise, so much movement, so much shouting and crying and tears. What kind of church was this? Everyone around me seemed so excited. All I felt was a heavy weight in my chest, like I was breathing in lead.

Stanyard's voice broke through the chaos. "We should go up there."

"What?" I turned to him.

"We should get prayer." He was fidgeting, his face and hands twitching as if he'd been tased. I'd never seen him like that, like he'd lost the ability to stand still, and it only fed my anxiety.

Suddenly, he seemed to regain control of his body. He straightened and drew his shoulders back. "I'm going."

He took two steps—then stopped and turned around. "Come with me."

"What?" I gasped again.

"Come with me," he repeated.

I gripped the straps of my backpack. "Stanyard, I don't... I can't..."

"Come on, we won't get another chance. You need this as much as I do."

"What's that supposed to mean?" I squawked. I felt like I should feel offended, but I just felt terrified. There was no way I was going up there, in front of all these people.

"Come on, they've got a bunch of people up there, praying for everyone. Let's go." Stanyard looked over his shoulder towards the front. I saw the tension in his body and knew he was about to run and leave me behind.

And for once, I wished he would.

"You go, then," I said, drawing back.

"No, if we go, we go together."

I started and looked up at him. He turned back to face me and shifted his feet, posture firm.

"I want you to come with me," he said, and held out his hand.

I stared at it, memories of screams and sirens and tears ricocheting in my head.

Phil, if you don't come now, I'll leave you behind!

I looked up into his face.

His dark eyes met mine, open and unafraid. "I won't go without you."

Give me a chance.

I reached out and grabbed his hand.

He gripped my fingers and dragged me into the crowd. He swam through the throng like he knew what he was doing as people instinctively parted to let us through. I hung onto his hand like a rope, afraid that if I let go I would drown.

The sound grew deafening as we neared the stage, but it wasn't because of the music. If anything, the rickety drums and screeching guitar grew warped and distant as the thrumming inside my head drowned everything out. My heart was pounding, and my ears were ringing, and my lungs were burning with a pressure that was both familiar and foreign at the same time.

What's going on?

Everything shattered when we broke through to the front. There was a gap between the crowd and the stage, and the void seemed cavernous. I suddenly felt like I was alone, even though Stanyard still held my hand. A cold breeze swept across the concrete, and I felt weak, chilled, and exposed.

If God had been there a moment ago, I couldn't feel Him now.

Stanyard abruptly let go of my hand. I turned to him in a panic. Pastor DeMarcus had him by the shoulders, his face to his.

"You know you're forgiven, right?" Pastor DeMarcus declared, voice as authoritative as it was quiet.

Stanyard started to say something, then changed his mind and swallowed instead.

Pastor DeMarcus shook him gently. "Why are you still trying to earn it?"

"I don't… I'm not…" Stanyard stuttered, then finally settled on, "I'm sorry."

His voice cracked in a way I'd never heard before, and I started to panic.

Pastor DeMarcus smiled. "He doesn't want a slave. He wants a *son*."

Stanyard shattered. He collapsed, and the pastor let him fall. Stanyard dropped to his knees and started to *cry*, the sobs raw and unashamed.

I gaped at him, feeling like my world was crumbling out beneath me. The Stanyard I knew would never let anyone see him cry. He was cold and stoic and sarcastic, and that was safe.

This wasn't safe.

This can't be God, can it?

Pastor DeMarcus stepped towards me. I tried to back away, but there was nowhere to go. *No, please don't*, I wanted to beg, but I couldn't find the words.

He smiled at me—a soft, gentle gesture that was completely dissonant from the violent noise in the room. "No, he's not safe. But He's good."

I flinched. "How did you—"

"He's already given you everything you need," he continued as if he hadn't heard me. "But you have to let go."

"Let go of what?"

He didn't answer. He'd already moved on to the person next to me, leaving me feeling like I'd missed an opportunity I could never get back.

The thrum continued unabated, each song seeming to have no beginning and no end. The singing and the praying and the drumming swirled into a homogenous beat, until I couldn't distinguish one from the other.

Everyone seemed to be having an experience except me. There was moaning and crying and dancing and speaking in tongues. Even Stanyard was lost to the world as he beat the ground with his fists.

I felt nothing. The only thing I heard was my own anxiety chattering; the only thing I could sense was the ache in my head and the burn in my ribs. What was wrong with me? Everyone around me was passionately in love with a God I wasn't even sure I knew. Why wasn't He speaking to me? Was He mad at me?

Nic was. Dad would be, when he thawed out. Surely God was grieved with the mess I'd made of things.

This is all my fault.

I don't know how long I stood there in silence, wishing God would say something and yet fearing what He would say if He did.

Finally, I turned around and walked away.

14

I left the tunnel and collected my devices from the guard. Shoving past a cluster of latecomers, I climbed the stairs until I found a floor of the parking garage that was deserted. As soon as the door shut behind me, cutting off the distant music, my anxiety broke. My pulse slowed, and I took a full breath.

I couldn't decide whether to be grateful or guilty. Since when had I been relieved to get out of *church*?

I shoved the thoughts aside and strode for the railing. I needed fresh air.

The ledge was wide enough to sit on, so I carefully climbed up and swung my legs over. I was three stories up, and the height should have terrified me, but there were too many other emotions competing in my head to leave room for acrophobia.

I leaned my head against the cool pillar and closed my eyes. I counted down, willing the throbbing behind my temples to slow. I focused on the breeze and a distant car horn and the omnipresent sound of traffic—anything but the chaotic singing and frantic praying that still echoed in my ears.

You have to let go.

Let go of what? The whole reason we were in this mess was because I had been careless. If I'd been more aware, or prepared, or in control of the situation, Dad would still be alive.

But I hadn't, and he wasn't, and there was no one else I could trust to fix it. No one on this planet, anyway.

"Phil! Where are you?" It was Stanyard, his shout echoing up the stairwell.

I groaned and sat up. The door slammed, and his sneakers squeaked on the asphalt as he ran to me. "Phil! Get down!"

"I wasn't going to jump," I groused, but I swung my legs back around. He grabbed my arm and helped me down.

He let go as soon as my feet were on solid ground. "What's wrong? I got up and you were gone, and Ephesus hadn't seen you leave…"

"It's fine, I'm sorry," I said, even though I didn't mean either statement. "I just had a headache."

"Anything I can do?"

"Take me back to base."

He searched me. "Okay."

We collected Ephesus and walked back to the car. Both boys were silent during the drive. I watched Ephesus in the rearview mirror and wondered what he thought of the service, but he seemed fine, relaxed even. Whatever the problem was, it was apparently only with me.

Jayde met us at the door. "You're late."

I glared at him. I wasn't in the mood to talk to him, much less receive orders from him.

Stanyard came to my defense. "I didn't realize she ran on your schedule."

Jayde ignored the comment. He gestured at me and started leading the way down the hall. "There's someone here to see you."

I reluctantly followed him back to the lab, the boys a step behind me. We came around the corner to see a tall, dark-haired man standing over Dad's tube, and I recognized him instantly.

"Tower!"

He turned. He looked so different up close. When he was two stories high in his lookout, it was hard to tell how old he was; now, I could see that he was only a few years younger than my dad. His sunken eyes were framed with crow's feet, and his unruly mop of hair was graying underneath. His skin was hardened from years of working in the sun, his knuckles bashed and scarred.

"Phil," he acknowledged, his hands finding a home in the pockets of his army pants.

Ephesus stepped into the room. "So you're Tower."

Tower studied him up and down, eyes lingering. "To her, yes. To you, I should be Bart."

I looked to Ephesus in alarm. "You guys know each other?"

Ephesus shook his head. I could see the gears ticking behind his eyes, but his face remained blank.

"You don't remember me, do you?" If Tower was disappointed, he wasn't showing it.

Ephesus shrugged. "Should I?"

"Not if your father had any say in it. It has been..." He frowned at me. "How old are you again?"

"Seventeen."

"Seventeen years," Tower finished. "But I always was the cool uncle."

My whole world bottomed out and then sprung back again like a rock on a trampoline.

"Uncle Bart?" Ephesus croaked.

Tower acknowledged him with a nod. "Nephew."

I watched the emotions play out on Ephesus's face and wondered if that was what I had looked like when *he* came back from the dead.

As for me, I couldn't even conjure up the energy to be surprised, and apparently, neither could Stanyard. "Next we'll find out you've got an evil twin," he muttered.

I glanced back at them where they waited in the doorway. Jayde shrugged. "It was news to me too."

Ephesus sputtered like a broken sprinkler. "I thought you were dead!"

Tower wrinkled his nose. "Is that what your father told you?"

"I mean, not in so many words, but…"

"And what about you?" Tower arched an eyebrow at me.

I shrugged. "I mean, Mom talked about you sometimes, but…" I knew Mom had a brother, but she hadn't seen him since before I was born. My parents had always spoken about him in past tense, so I'd assumed he was either dead or didn't care about us.

My dad had strongly implied it was the latter.

"Jerk," Tower muttered.

"But why didn't you tell me?" I demanded. "I was there, on Rott, and you said nothing. You had access to my file. You knew who I was."

He shrugged. "I didn't want you to worry."

I crossed my arms. "Well, let me make up for lost time."

He eyed me with a look that wasn't quite affectionate. "Okay, Q," he snarked. "Forgive me for not wanting to see you cry at my funeral."

"What?"

He took his hand out of his pocket to scratch his neck. "Don't take this the wrong way, but I didn't expect your plan with the virus to work—not that well. I knew that if my superiors reviewed the logs, it wouldn't take a detective to realize I'd let a whole floor of prisoners out of their cells."

I replayed our interactions in my mind—the long, contemplative looks I had thought so little of at the time. "So when I asked you to help…"

I was asking you to die.

He studied me from somewhere under his mop of hair. "It was a sacrifice I was willing to make."

I shivered. "Thank you," I said, and it felt wholly inadequate.

Ephesus's internal processor seemed to have rebooted. "But what are you doing here now, after all this time?"

Tower straightened. "I heard Blue Fire needed my help."

I flinched.

"And it looks like Catalyst does too." He looked down at Dad and made the sign of the cross.

"You're Catholic?" I asked.

"One of the many reasons your father and I didn't get along." Tower reached inside his jacket and pulled out a rosary. He slid it over his head and laid it across the top of Dad's tube.

I tracked the obvious implications. "Does that mean Mom…"

"Yes, before your father and the Bible-thumping Baptists got ahold of her."

The distaste was palpable in his voice, and Ephesus laughed. It was a genuine sound that brought a little life back into the room.

Tower tapped the machine's control panel. "No luck cracking the passcode?"

"No," Ephesus sighed. "Our best bet right now is extracting the memory dump, but the OS is completely foreign to me."

"I put a request out yesterday asking for any code anyone had," Stanyard said from the hall. "I got a few responses, but I don't know if any of it is useful."

"Worth a shot," Ephesus muttered, in a voice that suggested he was prepared to fail. "Let's go look. I'll be right back."

The latter statement was directed at me, which I acknowledged with a nod. He turned to Tower. "Thanks for coming back."

Tower clapped his shoulder. "We'll talk more later."

Ephesus nodded and left, taking Stanyard and Jayde with him.

Tower waited until they were out of sight down the hall before turning to me. "You know why I'm here, right?"

"What?"

"As happy as I am to see you, I didn't come here for a family reunion."

The severity of his tone sucked all the warmth out of the air, and suddenly, I knew what this was about. "Jayde called you, didn't he?"

He nodded.

I folded my arms over my chest and pinched my eyes shut. "You think I should do it. You think I'm the next 'Blue Fire.'"

"And you don't?"

My eyes flew open, startled by the question.

His sunken eyes searched me. "Why not you?"

I gaped at him. He of all people should understand. "You know why. You were *there*. I heard the radio conversation. I know what happened."

He looked down at the frozen glass coffin beside him. "And what do you think happened?"

I swallowed and forced myself to speak the painful truth. "I think Operation Blue Fire was a failure. I think it's my dad's fault Mom is dead."

"And I think it's mine."

I looked up at him. There was no grief on his face as he stared into Dad's tube, but his words were stretched, each syllable labored.

"I was supposed to pick up the drive that day. But I postponed the drop because there were whispers—I thought someone might be on to me."

He pressed his clenched fist to the frosted glass. "I could tell your dad was nervous about it, but I ignored him. Like I always did."

I bit my lip.

"Next thing I know, there's a call for an ambulance, and Thomas doesn't check into work, and no one's answering the radio, and my sister is dead."

He slammed his fist down with a crack. He bent over, his matted hair hiding the tears I could clearly hear in his voice.

"I should never have let him be in charge of the files!" he shouted. "I should have known he'd get caught. I should have known he wouldn't tell Abi."

"Why didn't he?" I whispered, the accusation piercing the air between us.

"Same reason he didn't tell you why she died." Tower planted both hands on the tube and pushed himself up. "To protect you."

"A lot of good that did," I snapped, and regretted it. I gagged as the guilt and fear clogged my stomach.

"I didn't say it worked."

I pressed the heels of my hands to my eyes to stop the tears from falling.

Tower turned to face me. "Your dad made mistakes, Phil. But so did I. I should have come and got you that day. I could have picked you up at school and had you out of town before Ambrose even knew what was happening. None of this—Red Rain, Mars, Rott—would have happened if I'd gotten you out."

I tried to imagine a version of my life where I hadn't grown up in a concentration camp. A version where I'd been rescued and protected. A version where someone, anyone, had stood up to Ambrose. But I couldn't.

"I shouldn't have given up on you. I shouldn't have given up on my family." Tower's gaze wandered again, and the penance in his voice offered the apology it was too late to give. "And I never should have given up on Blue Fire."

His eyes returned to mine, and I saw the truth I wanted so badly to deny. "You don't think Dad should have quit."

"No," he said, unashamed. "I don't."

When I didn't answer, he rolled up the sleeve of his jacket. He licked his finger and rubbed it on the inside of his arm, right above the elbow. A layer of thick foundation peeled away, revealing a tattoo I knew all too well.

He held it out for me to see. "We could have done it then. We can do it now. All we need is a voice."

It was my turn to look away as all my excuses died on my lips. My arguments suddenly seemed fragile and frail, but I couldn't push past the fog of fear that surrounded my mind like the containment camp walls.

"I don't—I won't want to," I managed finally.

"Then don't."

I looked back up at him.

His eyes were reserved behind the shadow of his hair. "If you're going to do it, it has to be your choice. I'm not here to convince you."

"Then why are you here?" I challenged.

"To remind you that you're not alone."

If that was his goal, it wasn't working. I felt more alone and confused than ever before. Why couldn't anyone understand why I didn't want to do this?

He didn't seem to expect a response. He pushed his sleeve back down and strode towards the door. "I'll be in the command center if you need me."

I watched him leave, too afraid to give a definitive goodbye. "How long are you staying?"

"As long as you are." He paused in the doorway. "If you do it…" The emphasis was on the "if," but barely. "If you choose to become Blue Fire, promise me one thing."

I steeled myself. "What?"

"Don't make the same mistake your father did."

"Which one?" I said, and winced.

He glanced over his shoulder. "Call me more than once a decade."

I searched his face.

"Your father and I were enemies." His eyes took one last look at the tube before returning to me. "But you and I don't have to be."

Then without waiting for a response, he turned the corner and left.

15

Ephesus returned a few minutes later with Stanyard, and they rigged up their various computers and devices. It was a horribly complicated process that quickly fizzled into inglorious failure. They modified and patched and rewrote their program again and again, and each time it coughed up more errors.

After a few hours of misery, Stanyard slammed his laptop shut and stood up to pace. Ephesus raked his hand through what was left of his hair. "What about patching into the circuit board?"

Stanyard shook his head. "Same problem—all their circuitry is proprietary."

"But you've done some hardware hacking before, haven't you? Can't you at least try—"

"Yeah, but nothing like this. If I pry this thing open, I'll have no idea what I'm looking at." He jabbed his finger at the machine. "What if I cross the wrong wire? I can't play with your dad's life like that."

The frustration evaporated from his muscles, leaving him looking deflated. "I'm sorry," he said, voice bent towards me. "I'm not good enough."

I wanted to comfort him, but I didn't know what to say. There was nothing I could say that would make this any better.

Ephesus didn't say it, but I could read it on his flushed face: We were running out of options. The boys couldn't hack around it, and we couldn't keep trying random passwords. We would soon exhaust the codes Nic had given us, and then we'd be back to square one, picking away at mathematically infinite possibilities.

Meanwhile, the longer Dad stayed under, the more damage he would suffer—until, at some point, he may as well just stay frozen.

Ephesus kicked me out of the lab and told me to go eat a late lunch. I begrudgingly obliged. Then, wanting to avoid everyone, especially Jayde, I found an abandoned office and curled up in a desk chair with the Bible Stanyard had given me.

I fanned the pages, looking for answers. I didn't find any, but at least it distracted me until it was time to go back to the Vons.

I walked back to the lab. I came around the corner to find Stanyard lying face-first on the floor.

My heart shot to my throat, and I started to call out to him—but then he moved. I hung back around the edge of the doorway as he picked himself up and sat cross-legged next to Dad's tube. His face and eyes were red, but it didn't look like he'd been crying. He sat there for a long minute, gaze in another universe.

I was just about to say something when he spoke.

"God, please. I don't know what to do."

He broke off into mutters, much of which wasn't English. He ran his hand along Dad's tube—then made a fist and pounded it into the floor.

"God, save him, please, for Phil's sake. You know it will kill her if he dies. And she's been through so much already. You have to save him—save *her*."

I slid my hand over my mouth.

His bloodshot eyes went to the ceiling and lingered there. When he spoke again, his voice was an unfiltered whisper.

"I'm worried about her."

I gripped the doorframe, desperate to say something. I wanted to reassure him, tell him that he didn't have to worry about me, that there was nothing to be concerned about. He didn't have to take care of me.

But none of those statements were true, and I knew it.

Stanyard started muttering again. I watched him as he bent over, hands raking his unruly hair, and tried to assimilate the man on the lab floor with the moody, impenetrable boy I thought I knew.

The Stanyard I'd gone to school with would never pray for me, not like this. He would never have given me a paper Bible. He would never have invited me to church. And he would never, ever have wallowed on the prayer floor and let me see him cry. The Stanyard I used to know never opened up to anybody, not even God.

And certainly not me.

I'm giving you my weapons, Phil.

I eased away from the door until I was out of sight of the lab windows. Then I turned and fled down the hall, careful to be light on my feet.

Tower took me home. I made him drop me off a few blocks away; the last thing I needed was Mrs. Von asking questions about Tower's muddy military jeep.

Thankfully, I was home before five, so Mrs. Von didn't have any questions. I went through our dinner routine and then managed to concoct a reasonable excuse to get out of watching TV. I escaped to Cea's bedroom and took my tablet off the charger.

It exploded in a shower of notifications, all of which were from Nic.

He had sent me more batches of codes throughout the day, which made me wonder when he had slept. His first few messages were simply business, but when I'd failed to respond—even though my tablet clearly showed as being online—his tone had turned from informative to interrogative to downright antagonistic.

DID YOU RECEIVE MY LAST MESSAGE?

IT'S CUSTOMARY TO ACKNOWLEDGE PEOPLE WHEN THEY'RE ASSISTING YOU

IF THERE'S BEEN AN ISSUE, I NEED TO KNOW. PREFERABLY IMMEDIATELY

DO I NEED TO SEND SARDIS?

ANDROMEDA VERITY NOLAN, IF YOU DON'T ANSWER MY MESSAGES, I SWEAR I WILL GROUND YOU FOR A MONTH

Who on Mars is Verity? I thought, before realizing it was probably Andromeda's middle name. It was no doubt on my file; I'd just never bothered to look it up.

The fact that Nic had was both hilarious and terrifying.

I typed back.

SORRY, I DIDN'T HAVE MY TABLET WITH ME

I watched his avatar flicker green as he came online. I was not at all surprised by his next words.

CALL ME

I obeyed and decided to save myself some trouble by initiating video.

He appeared, posed perfectly in the center of the frame with his arms crossed, like he'd been waiting all day for me to call. When he didn't offer any greeting, I sighed and answered the implied question. "I left my tablet at home, sorry."

"But you were online all day. And watching the most *inane* movies. I expected better of you, although at this exact moment I'm not sure why."

"Yeah, Ephesus installed a program that makes it look like 'Andromeda' is relaxing at home. Sorry, I forgot to tell you."

"I'm sensing a trend here." He unfolded his arms. "And what were you doing all day where you didn't need your tablet?"

"I'm not supposed to have registered electronics on base."

I could tell by the slant of his eyebrows that he didn't like that anymore than I did. "Stanyard and Ephesus are there the whole time," I added, desperate to reassure him, or me, or someone.

"Neither of those names brings me any comfort," he grunted. "But at least now I know you're not dead."

His expression relaxed, and I let out my breath. Even though there were only about three muscles that distinguished Nic's disgruntled face from his default one, I could tell the difference, and it made me a lot less nervous when he wasn't tense.

He picked up his coffee mug. "You're still grounded. As soon as you get home, you're not leaving your room for a month."

I acknowledged that with a humorless chuckle. "At this point, that sounds like a vacation."

He studied me. "What's wrong?"

"Nothing," I muttered, entirely out of habit.

He slammed his mug on the desk with a crack so loud I nearly dropped my device. "Do you think I'm stupid?"

The anger had returned to his voice, so the only response I could squeak out was, "Huh?"

He leered at the camera. "Do you honestly believe I'm going to fall for that?"

I threw up one hand in surrender. "Fall for what?"

"A woman who is 'fine' is, statistically speaking, the exact opposite. And you haven't been 'fine' in…" he glanced at his watch, "at least two months. So start talking."

I cringed. "I don't… want to," I fudged, which wasn't the truth, but it was at least closer to it.

"I don't care. I've got a fresh pot and all day. I'll wait." To demonstrate, he grabbed a carafe from somewhere out of frame and refilled his mug.

I stared at the screen, feeling cornered even though he was over a million miles away.

"Andromeda," he said, and it was a threat.

"Nic, I..." I mentally ran through all the things he didn't know, and all the anxiety and terror and confusion and *Jesus* of the last forty-eight hours crushed me like a load of bricks. My tears returned, hot and shameful, and I hid my face in my arm.

Nic let me sob for several minutes. "Phil."

I made a gasp that sounded like I'd been stabbed, appalled that he'd used my real name. I squinted at the screen through a veil of salty water.

His deep gray eyes searched mine. "Talk to me."

I gulped back another sob.

"I can't help you if you don't tell me what's going on."

Let me help you.

I pinched my eyes shut and waited until the world stopped spinning, anchored by the one fact that hadn't changed over the past week:

Nic could help me. And he would.

I coughed to clear the ugly tears from my voice and tried to decide where to start detangling the mess. "Well," I said, finally settling on the most bizarre revelation I had to share, "I've got an uncle."

"Living?"

"Yes," I replied, and then realized how hilarious that was. Without warning, all the anxiety of the past two days shattered into hysterical laughter. I dropped the tablet as I buckled over and howled. It sounded absolutely terrifying, but it felt so good.

Nic waited until I came up for air. "I take it your rib doesn't hurt anymore," he commented over the rim of his coffee cup.

I abruptly stopped when I realized he was right—it didn't hurt anymore. I lifted the hem of my shirt and looked at my side.

The bruise was gone.

Pain goes.

"Andi?" Nic questioned, the speaker muffled by the blankets.

"He healed me," I murmured.

"What?"

"He healed me," I repeated, louder, as if that could make it all make sense.

"He who? Look at me when I'm speaking to you."

"Sorry." I grabbed the tablet. "I don't know how to tell you this…"

"You never do."

"But…" I licked my lip and braced myself for the rejection. "Jesus healed me."

To my surprise, he didn't laugh. "Meaning…?"

"Just that," I said, gesturing with one arm. "A lady prayed for me today, and my bruise is gone. It doesn't hurt at all."

He blinked twice. "That wasn't what I was expecting you to say, but at least it's not bad news."

I opened my mouth, then changed my mind. He could take it or leave it. I knew what God had done for me.

"So." Nic shifted in his chair. "Bob's your uncle?"

I dragged my mind back to the present. "Actually, his name is Bart."

"That's even worse."

I parsed out the next words, watching for his reaction. "But we know him as Tower."

Nic wretched, gagging most of his mouthful back into his cup. "Tower is your *uncle*?"

"Eyup."

"Mom or dad's side?"

"Mom's."

"Weird but okay." He wiped his mouth on his sleeve. "Why didn't he tell you?"

"He didn't think he was going to make it off of Rott alive."

"Oh ye of little faith," Nic muttered, "but fair point." He drew his eyebrows together as he reprocessed everything I had just said. "I take it you never met him growing up."

I shook my head. "I knew Mom had family, but Dad always told me they were all dead."

Nic propped his elbow on the arm of his chair and put his chin in his hand. "And I thought I was the only one keeping skeletons in the closet."

I huffed. "You should sue for plagiarism."

"I'll add it to the list of complaints I have for our next parent-teacher conference." He leaned forward and tented his fingers. "Listen, I realize this would normally be considered in poor taste, but given the amount of resurrected family members you have, I need to ask..." He cleared his throat, and for a brief moment, the sarcasm left his voice. "Is your mom actually dead?"

"Yes," I whispered, "she is." I sighed, expecting tears, but instead I just felt *dry*.

He watched me carefully, eyes tracking like a cursor. "Did it happen like it says in her file?"

I swallowed. "Not exactly."

Nic waited.

I tried to force the words up my throat, but they kept catching there, thickened by the fear and the confusion and the guilt. He was going to be so mad when he found out I'd kept all this from him.

You have to let go.

But he needed to know. I needed him to know.

I sat up. "That's actually what I need to talk to you about."

"Hang on." He bent over out of frame, and I heard a drawer sliding on a track. There was rustling, and a second later he reappeared, notebook in hand. He crossed one leg over the other, leaned back in the chair, and clicked a pen open. "Continue."

I smiled and did as I was told.

I told him everything—about Dad, about the rebellion, about Operation Blue Fire. I told him about gun training, about talking to Mrs. Nolan, about finding the truth on my dad's phone. I told him about Tower and the real reason my mother was dead. I even told him about going to church and meeting John and Dowe. I held nothing back, and by the time I was done, I felt like I could breathe again.

He didn't say much, only interrupting to ask a couple of clarifying questions. Surprisingly, he had the most questions about Stanyard and the church, even though that was the most innocuous part of my story. When I was done, I sat back and gave him space to speak—but he didn't.

I waited until he'd finished scribbling in his notebook before prompting him. "Well?"

He arched his eyebrows but didn't look up.

"Don't you have an opinion?"

"Several passionate ones." He clicked his pen shut and tossed the notebook on the desk. "None of which I intend to share."

A fireball of frustration imploded in my chest. "Oh, so *now* you're deciding to mind your own business? I just told you they want me to lead a war, and you decide now's a good time to take a vow of silence."

He finally looked up and met my gaze. "Do you want me to tell you what to do?"

My next comeback died on my tongue. *Is that what I want?*

He didn't wait for me to decide. "Because I won't."

I clicked my teeth shut and waited.

"I won't tell you what to do, because based on past experience, that increases the probability that you'll do the exact opposite."

I flushed poppy red when I realized he was right.

"But." He lingered on the word as he refilled his mug. "I think you know what I would do."

When are you coming home?

"Yeah," I said quietly, eyes on my lap. "I do."

"Any progress on unlocking the tube?" he prodded, as if predicting my next objection.

I shook my head. "Ephesus still hasn't been able to hack the memory dump or whatever."

"Don't tell him I said this, but that surprises me." Nic blew on his cup of coffee and waited for the ripples to subside. "I guess

Carnegie really wanted to make sure no one else could get their hands on your father."

I grimaced. Nic was right, and in a cruel twist of fate, Carnegie had succeeded. Password-locking the tube ensured that if he couldn't have Red Rain, no one could.

"Do you have any idea who he was working with? Any idea what his plan was before you ingloriously ruined everything?"

I knew Nic was trying to make me feel less horrible, but it wasn't working. "None. He had his phone set to purge data every twenty-four hours…"

Time stopped when I remembered the one important conversation that was still on Carnegie's phone.

WHEN CAN I EXPECT DELIVERY?

Nic started to swear, then let the sound fizzle out into a hiss. "I can tell by the look on your face that I'm about to regret everything I just said."

"Yeah, probably." I gnawed on my lip and started calibrating all the ways my idea could go horribly wrong. There were dozens, but the more I thought about it, the more I realized it was my best chance.

I opened a note program to start writing things down—then stopped, closed my eyes, and did something I hadn't done in days.

Jesus, give me wisdom.

"Well?" Nic grunted.

I started. I'd almost forgotten he was there. "What?"

"If you're concocting another suicidal idea, I'd like to know what it is, so I can at least start prewriting your obituary."

The words were biting, but his expression was anything but. I searched his eyes and found the truth he could not say.

Talk to me.

I held his gaze. "I think I know how to get the code."

I told him my idea, walking through the details slowly until it was cemented in my own mind. He made a heroic effort to keep a rigid face during the whole conversation, but I saw the light behind his eyes flicker. He looked sad, which told me I was right: This was my only hope.

"Well?" I prompted when I'd finished.

He groaned and shifted in the chair, looking away from me for the first time since we'd started the call. "What did I just say about not telling you what to do?"

I grunted. We both knew I wasn't waiting for permission.

But we also knew that wasn't what I was really asking.

I chewed on my words until I could rearrange them into the truth. "Nic?"

His eyes returned to mine. "Yes, Andromeda?"

"Will you help me?"

16

"You want to go where?"

I slid into Stanyard's car and slammed the door. "Somewhere out of town. I need to connect to a cell tower that's nowhere near home—or base."

He hesitated, his hand on the gear shift. "Why?"

I buckled my seatbelt. "Just do it."

"Yeah no, I'm not playing that game." He took his hand off the wheel and leaned back in the seat. "If I'm going to drive you to the middle of nowhere, I need to know why."

I glared at him, but the frown on his face told me I'd have to try harder than that. I fingered the straps of my backpack. I hadn't planned on telling him what I was doing until it was over—mainly so that he didn't try to stop me.

"Come on, Phil, please," he said when the silence had grown long. "At least involve me if you're going to do something stupid."

Well, that's one way to put it.

I sighed. "Can I trust you?"

"Of course," he said, almost before I'd finished the question. "But do you?"

I stopped and looked at him. He let me search him, eyes wide and unbarred. When he spoke again, his voice was a gentle invitation. "Do you trust me?"

He held out his hand, and for the first time, I didn't see greasy alleys and flashing lights. I saw smoke and stained concrete, heard praying and chaotic singing. I saw the tears in his eyes and his fists beating the floor as he prayed, prayed for mercy. And through it all I saw his hand reaching out to me, begging me to share in an experience I didn't yet understand.

I won't go without you.

I looked back up into his face. "Yes, I do."

He smiled. "Okay." He put the car in gear and pulled away from the curb. "What are we doing?"

I unzipped my backpack and pulled out Carnegie's phone. "I need to make a call."

He slammed on the brakes, nearly sending me into the dash. I dropped the phone and braced myself. "Stanyard!"

"Sorry." He glanced in the review mirror to make sure no one was behind us on the street, then put the car back in park. "But if you're going to do what I think you are, I can't let you do that."

"I didn't ask." I fished the phone off the floor. "And it's my only hope."

He let out a long, rickety sigh. "Phil, those people want you dead."

"Yeah, and if I don't get that tube thawed, my dad will be. You said yourself we're running out of options." I shook the device at him.

He turned away from me and glared out the window, silent and stewing.

"If it will save him, I have to try. And I need you to drive me. I can't take the bus—Andromeda isn't supposed to be logging any activity away from home right now. And I know Jayde won't let me do it from base."

He still wouldn't look at me. I reached over and grabbed his knee. "Stanyard, please. I need your help."

He tensed, and so did I. He looked down at my hand, seemingly as shocked as I was that I'd put it there.

Slowly, he slid his hand under mine and entwined our fingers. I didn't pull away.

"All right," he said. He squeezed my hand, then let go to take the wheel. "But we need to make it quick. That's a registered device—they'll know as soon as you bring it online."

Nic had warned me about that, but it was a risk I was willing to take.

Stanyard copied my silence as he navigated rush hour traffic. It took over half an hour to reach a mall in the suburbs—somewhere far away from home, but busy enough that if they did trace the call, they'd have trouble figuring out who was responsible.

Stanyard parked on the edge of the lot. "Are you sure about this?"

For an answer, I turned Carnegie's phone on and handed it to him.

He didn't argue as he deftly navigated the settings with his thumbs. A few seconds later, he passed the device back to me. "It's online. Make it fast."

I opened Carnegie's texts and clicked on the most recent one.

YOU FOOL

Stanyard read over my shoulder and said nothing.

I took a deep breath, muttered a prayer, and dialed the number.

The line picked up after two rings.

"I thought you were dead."

Maybe it was because I'd had such a string of bad luck with men lately, but I was more than a little surprised to hear that it was a woman. She had a curt voice with perfect pronunciation, but there was a subtle Chinese clip to her words. The greeting was spoken with no affection at all, and while I knew she was talking about Carnegie, I realized the statement could equally apply to me.

I swallowed and forced my voice to be cold and confident—the same tone I used with Andes. "Funny, that's what I wanted you to think."

There was a sharp intake of breath and rustling. She'd lost the upper hand and with it her composure; her next words were harried and almost obscured by her natural Mandarin accent. "Who is this? How did you get this number?"

Stanyard gripped the gear shift, ready to move. I put my hand up and spoke calmly and clearly.

"This is Philadelphia Smyrna, and I believe I have something you want."

17

There was utter silence, and for a second I thought she'd hung up.

"Fascinating," she said finally. Her perfect English enunciation returned. "You really are a clever girl."

I winced. "So I've heard."

"Philadelphia." She rolled the name slowly, as if measuring how it fit me. She finished with a contemplative *hmm*, then continued. "To what do I owe the pleasure of this call?"

I put the phone on speaker. "I believe you're expecting a delivery."

"I was."

The past tense was definitive, as was the patient silence that followed.

I measured my words, making sure to repeat them exactly as Nic and I had rehearsed. "I apologize for the delay, but I'm hoping we can still make arrangements."

She barked a laugh so sharp it made me flinch. "Oh really?"

I swallowed. What if she called my bluff? I only had one shot at this. "Yes," I said, forcing myself to sound aloof and annoyed—

like the way Nic used to talk to me. "That is, if you're still buying."

"Oh, I am." She composed herself. "I just didn't think you were selling."

"You and I both know he's as good as dead in there," I snapped. The words felt bitter on my tongue, and the pain was not an act.

Stanyard touched my knee. I reached down and grabbed his hand, gripping it like the railing of a capsizing boat.

She was silent for a beat. "I'm sorry," she said finally.

I tried to weigh how genuine the condolence was, then decided it didn't matter. "So, what's he worth to you?"

"What do you want?" The question was honest.

"Money," I replied without hesitation. I was very grateful Nic had helped me plan what to say; I would never have been able to come up with a believable answer around the swirling in my stomach. "Enough to get far away from you."

She laughed again, a sarcastic tinkle this time. "Charmed. But I'm sure we can come to an arrangement. Bring the tube and I'll bring the money and a plausible excuse for transferring it to you. Do you want to set the meeting place, or shall I?"

"I—I will," I stuttered, a little startled that she'd agreed so quickly. "I will text you the details from this line by 1400. We meet tonight, or not at all."

"I would expect nothing less."

Stanyard tapped the dashboard clock with his other hand. I nodded. "And there's one more thing."

"Of course there is."

Jesus, please let this work.

I took a deep breath and molded my words to be cold and slippery. "You'd better come prepared to unlock the tube."

There was a pause, which told me all I needed to know: She knew Carnegie had password-locked the tube, and she had the code.

"Why do you care?" Her tone shifted, and I could tell I was losing her. So I did exactly what Nic had told me to do—avoid the question.

"You want him or not?" I droned, as if the whole thing were beneath me. "Because if you're not paying, there are plenty of other people who are. So unless you want me to sell Red Rain to the highest bidder, you'll unlock the tube while I'm watching."

"Philadelphia," she murmured, voice slick with admiration. "How mercenary of you."

"It's been a long week," I muttered. "Do we have a deal?"

"We certainly do. I will await your text." I heard the smile in her voice as she added, "I look forward to meeting you."

"The pleasure is all mine," I said, and hung up.

*

"You did what?"

I'm not sure who was more upset: Ephesus or Jayde. We'd gathered everyone, including Tower, Lev, and Mrs. Nolan, in the command center to tell them the plan, and now the entire room was staring at me in mortified silence. It took only seconds for both Ephesus and Jayde to go from shocked to irate, although each for completely different reasons.

"I can't believe you brought that phone online!" Jayde snapped, every muscle in his neck pinched.

"And you let her do it!" Ephesus reeled on Stanyard, flapping his sling like a disgruntled bird. "Why didn't you call me?"

Stanyard shrugged, and only I could see the smile in the corner of his lips.

I didn't have time for their theatrics; the woman was expecting meeting details in three hours. "You got a better idea?" I demanded, knowing full well that they didn't. "She has the code—this will work."

Jayde growled and gripped his hair in a way that looked painful. "We don't even know who this woman is! She could be the commander in chief of the United, and you want to meet her for coffee."

He wasn't entirely wrong, and given the fact that the lady was distinctly Asian, the chances of her being a top United official were high. But it didn't matter.

I had to save my dad.

"What if they capture you? They could torture you for information," Tower grunted in a way that suggested he had experience in such matters.

"He's right, we can't risk it," Jayde agreed. "There's no way they'll let you out of that room alive."

"Then I'll go alone," I snapped, and meant every word. "If they catch me, the worst that could happen is they read my prints and realize I'm going by Andromeda. They won't be able to trace me to the base—that's the whole reason I've stayed offline."

"They'll know about Nic and the Vons, though," Mrs. Nolan whispered.

I turned to her. "I know. I already talked to Nic. It's a risk I—we—are willing to take."

"Nic, if this doesn't work, and they—"

"At least I'll see them coming."

"Phil, please," Ephesus begged, pulling on every string of sibling affection he could find. "I can't let you do this."

"And yet you'd do the same thing if you thought it could save Dad." I grabbed his good hand and looked up into the chocolatey eyes I had trusted for so long. "If you help me, we can pull this off. I get to pick the meeting place. You can stake it out—surround the whole place with snipers if that makes you feel better." I directed the last sentence at Jayde.

He folded his arms across his chest and didn't relent.

Lev leaned close to his ear. "She's too valuable," he hissed, as if I weren't there.

"I'm not asking permission," I declared, loud enough for everyone to hear. I let go of Ephesus's hand and drew myself up. I spun a slow circle, trading glances with everyone in the room.

Two days ago, these people were willing to let me lead a rebellion. Couldn't they help me save one man's life?

"I'm going. We're going to set up a heist to get the code from this woman and save my father, and we're doing it tonight." I turned to look at Jayde again. "So unless you're prepared to lock 'Blue Fire' in a cell, I suggest you help me."

"I am," he said without hesitation, making me regret my choice of words. He unfolded his arms. "But I heard it didn't go well for the last two men who tried it."

Stanyard nearly choked on a laugh as he tried to stifle it.

Jayde made all his displeasure known in one slow, grumbling breath. "Well? What's your plan?"

Ephesus grabbed my shoulder. "You aren't really thinking of dragging Dad in there, are you?"

"No..." I said, my brain returning to all the problems I needed to solve. "But Nic had a suggestion about that."

Ephesus saw the look on my face and paled. "Oh no..."

Jayde arched an eyebrow.

I faced him. "How many bodies do you have in the morgue?"

He cast one final glance around at his troop. Tower nodded.

"Just the one," Jayde said, turning back to me. "But you're welcome to him."

18

Apparently nothing good happens in abandoned parking garages.

It was the second time in so many days that I'd been in one—and not the same one, which made me wonder how many there were in this city. But I could see why Jayde had chosen it as the meeting place: The split levels made it possible for his men to watch just out of sight, rifles ready. Several more crouched behind the concrete pillars on the other side of the room.

I stood alone in the middle of the floor, leaning against one of Jayde's SUVs. The boys had folded the seats down to make room for the coffin-sized glass tube. It lay there, crusted with frost, screen flashing an angry red as it counted down.

Our decoy was convincing. We'd bought—thanks to a connection of Andes's—an identical model. Stanyard and Ephesus had altered the control panel and rigged it with what was essentially a fancy credit card skimmer. When the woman typed the code on the screen, it would send the password to Stanyard's computer so he could input it on the real tube. If all went well, Dad's tube would be unlocked before the woman even realized she'd been scammed.

Of course, it would all be over if she looked too closely at the body in the ice. I hadn't watched while the boys dressed and froze Carnegie. I'd found an empty room to pray in and asked God to forgive me for desecrating the dead to save the living.

"We're live. Blue Fire, are you receiving?" Stanyard radioed in my ear.

The unwanted nickname was somehow even more vile coming from his lips; he had never called me anything but Phil, except in front of the Vons. But we were communicating over wireless, which could be intercepted, so Jayde had insisted on using callsigns.

I felt the microscopic transmitter with my finger. It fit neatly in my ear, almost invisible to passersby. "I hear you, Augustine."

"Remember, get the code and get out. The money is optional," Ephesus chimed in. He'd agreed, at the collective behest of Jayde and me, to stay behind and help monitor things from the command room. He'd volunteered to—more like insisted on—going in my place, but I wouldn't let him. This woman was expecting to meet me, and I wasn't about to scare her off by sending someone else.

"T-minus two minutes," Jayde said. I knew he was posed just out of sight on the level above me, the one who would be the first to shoot if this woman pulled anything.

"Car approaching," radioed an officer I didn't recognize. "Expensive, foreign make—guessing that's our target."

I turned and gave myself one last check in the car's side mirror. This woman knew me as Philadelphia, and I'd tried my best to bring that girl back. I wore a skirt I'd raided from Cea's closet and a drab military jacket one of Jayde's officers had loaned me. I'd removed my contacts and piercings and washed the makeup off my face. There hadn't been time to do anything with my hair, so I'd pinned it up under a scarf and hoped the woman wouldn't ask questions.

I looked like a prisoner of war more than anything else, but in a way, that's what Philadelphia had been.

Not anymore.

"Yup, I think that's her," the officer continued. "Chinese, early forties, and everything she's wearing costs at least ten grand."

"She parked a block away and is walking in," another confirmed. "She's alone. Definitely not dressed for combat."

Someone grunted, crackling the line. "She's either stupid or desperate."

"If we're lucky, she'll be both," Jayde said. "Let her in."

I closed my eyes and prayed. Stanyard did the same under his breath.

"She's coming up the elevator." Jayde's sigh clogged the line. "It's all on you, Blue Fire."

I opened my eyes and turned to face the elevator.

Holy Spirit, pave the way.

The light above the elevator flashed green, and the doors opened.

She looked exactly like I imagined she would. She was old enough to be my mother, not that you could tell with how flawless her skin was. She was about my height, with features that were somehow both sharp and curved at the same time. She had confident black eyeliner and bloodred lips, and her crisp white-on-black skirt set looked like it cost more than a small car. Her long, dark hair was done up in a sophisticated updo and fastened with pearls.

She stood in the doorway just long enough to take me in, then walked towards me, stiletto heels clipping on the concrete.

"You came," I said, not sure how else to initiate the conversation.

"Of course." She stopped in front of me and smiled. "Asia," she volunteered, and offered her hand.

I eyed it, then extended my scrutiny to her distinctly Chinese features.

She winked. "It's not my real name, but it was easier for the boys in Washington to remember."

I gingerly accepted the handshake. "Philadelphia."

She *tsked*. "I like Andromeda much better. It suits you."

I froze, my hand glued to hers with sweat. Someone on the radio cursed.

She mercifully released her grip. "Thames is—was—an old friend of mine. There's no reason to be afraid."

I took a slow step back. "Forgive me if I have trouble believing that."

"I understand. I know this whole ordeal has been very traumatic for you. You must believe me when I say it was never supposed to be this way." She gave me a slow once-over, expression thoughtful. "But I think you know that."

"That's what they tell me," I muttered, and waited.

Her eyes came to land on my scarf. "Can I see? What you did with your hair."

"Phil, don't—" Stanyard warned in my ear.

I reached up and undid the scarf. I pulled out the pin keeping the twist in place, and my ashy blonde locks tumbled to my shoulders.

Asia stretched a pale hand towards me. I didn't move. She used her impractically-long manicured fingernails to detangle my sweaty kinks.

"Hmm," she murmured. "Needs some toner, but I like it. It's a good color for you." She stepped back until there was a socially acceptable distance between us. "If you need a good hairdresser, I have one in Beacon Hill I can recommend."

"I'll keep that in mind," I said. I weighed her tone and tried to decide where she fit on the spectrum of my enemies.

"Don't let her stall," Jayde hissed on the line.

"Right," I acknowledged them both. "Shall we?" I stepped back and gestured at the car.

"Yes, of course." She opened her pocketbook and pulled out a phone. "I have the money ready to send. I've categorized it as an appearance fee—so if anyone asks, you spoke at a conference for entrepreneurial young women for me. Something about overcoming the challenges of being recently assimilated to start your own business."

"How charming."

She shrugged. "It's my favorite way to launder money. Shall I send it?" She showed me the screen.

"First, code." I opened the passenger door so she could easily access the keypad.

Her eyes glinted as she smirked. "As you wish."

She stepped up to the car and keyed in a code. The access panel flashed up a loading screen—a feature installed by Ephesus to give us a delay.

Jayde had a backup plan if the woman gave us a bogus code. But I didn't like how his plan ended.

I gripped the car door, praying fiercely.

Oh God, please save my dad.

I listened for confirmation from Stanyard, but the silence on the line was deafening. He should have tried the code by now. Was something wrong? What if the wireless malfunctioned and he hadn't gotten the password?

"Did it work?"

I started and looked up at Asia.

She smiled. "Did it work? Because if not, there's one other number I can try."

The blood was pounding so loudly in my ears that I barely heard Stanyard's shout of victory.

"We're in!"

Asia laughed. "Don't look so surprised, honey. I know this is a setup. I know you have friends listening."

The line erupted in barked orders. Ephesus started yelling at me to get out of there.

I pulled the transmitter out of my ear and held it up for Asia to see.

She winked. "I knew that if I allowed you to pick the meeting place, you'd come with backup. You can assure your friends I'm unarmed. I have no intention of hurting you."

I believed her, but that opened up more questions than it answered. "Then why did you agree to come?"

She spread her hands. "I wanted to meet you. And besides, you needed the code, didn't you?" She rapped the tube with her knuckles. "This is a rather impressive decoy, though. I do hope you don't have a real body in there."

"It's Carnegie," I answered. "He's yours if you want him."

In my peripheral, I saw one of Jayde's men slide around a pillar and aim his gun at Asia. I put up a hand to stop him.

Asia rolled her eyes and didn't bother to turn around. "Yet another mess of his I have to clean up. Did the code work?"

"Yes," I said. "And thank you."

The soldier lowered his gun.

"Of course," Asia crooned. "You know, you could have saved yourself all these theatrics if you'd just asked me for the code. I would have given it to you."

"Really?" It was a challenge.

"Absolutely. I never wanted to freeze your father. I never needed him in the first place. Red Rain was Carnegie's obsession." She picked a stray hair off her tailored suitcoat. "Melting cities with acid rain? Too messy for my tastes. And I can't *stand* unnecessary messes."

"But Carnegie was going to sell him to you," I argued, remembering the texts.

She shrugged. "Sometimes we compromise for our allies."

Carnegie had said the same thing to me—and I abruptly realized I had no idea where their tangled alliance of deception began and ended.

I knew Jayde must be screaming at me on the radio, but this might be my only chance to get answers. "If you're so benevolent, why not just give me the code over the phone? Do you know how much time we've wasted setting this up? I could have had my dad thawed by now."

She was unashamed. "Would you have agreed to meet me otherwise?"

"No," I admitted.

"That's all I wanted, Andromeda—a chance to see you face to face. I knew as soon as you got the code, you'd disappear back to Mars, and we'd never speak again. So when you called, I knew it was my only chance to meet you and give you this."

She reached back into her pocketbook and withdrew a jewelry box. "Happy birthday, a few weeks early."

She held it out. I didn't take it. "Birthday?"

"Did you know Andromeda's birthday is July 25th? That also happens to be the date of some big, boring state dinner we're all obliged to attend. Thames was going to bring you along. We all joked it was your coming out party."

I imagined a ballroom filled with flowing dresses and immaculate suits—and Thames flaunting me like a trophy as he introduced me to all the officials who wanted my people dead.

I shivered. "Who's 'we'?"

She ignored the question. She opened the jewelry box and admired the contents. "I'll admit, I'm disappointed you won't be making it. I was looking forward to inducting you into high society. Cynthia—Mrs. Nolan and I had arranged a day out on the town dress-shopping, the spa, everything."

She snapped the box shut and looked back up at me. "It's not too late, you know. You can still come with me. There's a mansion in Back Bay with your name on it."

The thought that I might have inherited more than money from the Nolans never occurred to me—but it all seemed irrelevant. "Last I checked, the United had several warrants out for my arrest," I reminded her.

She laughed. "I am the United. You let me deal with the boys in Beijing."

"Thames seemed pretty afraid of the boys in Beijing," I commented, memories of his anguished cries and the fatal gunshot echoing in my ears.

"Thames was a coward, I'm sorry to say," Asia declared with anything but remorse. "But you're not, are you?"

I frowned at her.

"You're not a coward, Andromeda. If you were, you wouldn't be here. You'd still be on Mars."

I should still be on Mars.

She reached out and pinched the sleeve of my army jacket with her fingers. Her face contorted in a grimace. "You don't belong here, Andromeda. You're not one of them."

"Them?"

You want to do this? You have to learn to be like us.

She gestured at the floor above us where Jayde and his men were hiding. "All this scheming and fighting and scrabbling in the dark like rats. You're not a terrorist."

But I don't want to do this. I'm not like you.

"Thames said I was."

She spread her hands. "All part of the PR. The media lies about everything, and your life story is no exception. But I know the real you, Andromeda."

"Do you?" I wasn't even sure I knew myself, not anymore.

"You're a Nolan." She laughed, as if it were that simple. "You're one of us now. You don't belong down here, on the street. You belong with us, in Washington, in Beijing."

Beijing was the last place I belonged.

Asia held out her hand. "Come with me, Andromeda."

Come with me.

I slid back. "Maybe you're right. Maybe I'm not one of them. But I'm definitely not one of you."

I expected her to be offended by the slight, but I was disappointed. She just smiled, coyly, as if that was the answer she had been hoping for. "As you wish. At least take this." She held the box out again. "Please, I picked it out for you."

When I hesitated, she chuckled. "It won't explode or anything. That would be an unnecessary mess."

I slowly took the box and opened it.

A single strand of pearls lay on a bed of blue velvet. Underneath the necklace was tucked a linen calling card embossed with silver gilding.

"If you ever need anything in the future, please, call me directly. You're a friend of the family now, which means my line is always open to you."

I fingered the necklace and didn't answer.

She pulled her phone out and tapped a button. "I sent the money—to help with revival costs."

I stared, unsure whether to thank her or run for my life.

"I really am sorry about what happened. When he gets through therapy, I would appreciate a call letting me know that he survived."

"Sure," I said, even though I had no intention of doing any such thing. I closed the box.

"Well, my driver is waiting. Thank you for meeting me. It was a pleasure." She turned and walked towards the elevator.

"Goodbye," I declared, not with any affection—desperately hoping that the words would be the end of our relationship.

"Goodbye, Andromeda." She stepped into the elevator and called her floor. "Oh, will you tell Cynthia that I miss our coffee dates?" She pressed the button to hold the door. "Tell her I can make this all go away. I can have her file cleared. All she has to do is call me."

She didn't wait for me to acknowledge that. She stepped back and allowed the doors to close. "Until we meet again, Andromeda."

She winked as the doors sealed shut.

19

When we got back to base, I was crushed to find that Dad was still very much frozen.

"It's going to take time," Mrs. Nolan said. She'd transformed back into a nurse, scrubs and all, and was sanitizing a new machine with gloved hands. "We have to bring him to temperature slowly, and then he has to be placed in stasis while we work on him."

She knocked on the machine with her knuckles. It looked like a giant incubator. The side was crusted with control panels and buttons, and an octopus of wires and tubes dangled from it.

"This machine will essentially do the living for him while we replace his damaged organs. Once we're sure he's viable and everything is functioning independently, then, *and only then*, will we be able to bring his brain online and work on bringing him to consciousness."

I walked over to Dad's tube and peered through the ice. Dad's face was still frozen in agony, but for the first time, the sight didn't fill me with horror. For the first time in days, there was hope—hope my father would be coming back.

I put my palm on the glass. "I'm sorry, Dad," I whispered one last time. "But it's going to be okay."

Mrs. Nolan stripped her gloves. "It's going to take at least seventy-two hours to bring him back to temperature. And most of that time will just be spent monitoring the machine while it does the work." She gestured at the control panel, which glowed yellow and displayed a chaotic readout.

I spun around. "Will you stay with him?"

She tipped her head to the side and waited.

"Someone has to supervise all the technicians and make sure everything's getting taken care of. I can't be here all the time, and you know more about this than me." I looked into her eyes. "He needs a doctor."

She smiled. "I'd be honored."

"Thank you," I said, and returned the gesture.

She went back to prepping the machine. I watched her in silence for a minute. "There is something I need to tell you."

She acknowledged me with a busied *hmm* as she grabbed a cloth and wiped the outside of the glass.

"Asia wanted me to pass along a message."

I saw her hand tighten around the rag, but she did not look up. "And what did she say?"

"That she misses your coffee dates." I pondered the next words before spitting them out. "And that she can make this all go away, if you just call her."

"I'll keep that in mind," she said in a tone as walled as a prison. "Anything else?"

I rolled Asia's invitation around in my mind, debating how much I wanted to share. "I guess my birthday is July 25th."

"It is. That was my mother's birthday."

"And apparently there's a state dinner that was supposed to be my coming out party."

Mrs. Nolan gave up any pretense of working as she stared at her reflection in the glass. "We talked about it."

"She says I don't belong here," I continued. I had to know how much of Asia's story was the truth—and how much Mrs.

Nolan agreed with her. "She says I belong with them, in Washington. That I'm one of you now."

Mrs. Nolan finally turned and looked back at me. Her face was straight, devoid of any criticism or longing. "You were supposed to be."

She didn't offer anything more, perhaps because there was nothing else to say.

I stayed with Dad all night and into the morning. I'd called the Vons and told them I was sleeping over at a friend's house, and then called again several more times throughout the evening in an attempt to reinforce that fact. There was no telling whether or not they'd remember, but it would have been too late to take me home by the time we got back from meeting Asia.

So I stayed by my dad's side through the next day, praying and watching as Mrs. Nolan and Ephesus monitored the machine's progress. Mrs. Nolan claimed the procedure was going well, but I couldn't see any change yet. Some of the frost on the glass had turned into condensation, but inside the cryoprotectant still looked as solid as ever.

Ephesus convinced me to go home for the night. After all, the sleepover excuse probably wouldn't work a second time.

I went to find Stanyard. I'd seen him a few hours ago, but he'd wandered off, saying he had programming to do. Something about disguising the power drain from the defrost procedure. I searched the base from top to bottom and even asked several strangers where he was, but no one had seen him or Tower.

Someone finally directed me to Jayde.

"I sent them on an errand," he said without any more explanation. "I can take you home."

I inwardly grimaced and hoped the gesture didn't make it onto my face. "I'll wait."

Jayde shrugged and glanced at his watch. "Suit yourself, but you'll be at least an hour late getting home."

I weighed my choices: I could be stuck in a car with Jayde, or I could spend my entire evening putting the Vons back together.

I chose the former.

Lev came with us. We took Jayde's giant black SUV, and I begrudgingly accepted shotgun when Lev offered it to me. Mercifully, neither man was feeling conversational, so I spent the ride looking out the window and trying to pray.

It was going to be a long month—or more—while we revived Dad. Nic said we should leave as soon as Dad was viable, but there was no telling how long it would take just to get him breathing on his own. Should I have his prints altered while he was in surgery? What if he needed memory care like the Vons had? I wasn't ready to admit that my father might lose his mind, but it was a possibility I had to consider. Was there someone on Mars that could do neurotherapy if we went home?

I was jostled out of my thoughts when Jayde slammed on the brakes to avoid someone merging lanes. "Sorry," he offered.

I looked around and abruptly realized that we'd been driving for longer than usual—and we were nowhere I recognized. I sat up. "Where are we?"

"There's something you need to see," Jayde said, and my blood ran cold.

Jesus, help.

I grabbed the door handle. "Stop the car."

Without taking his eyes off the road, he reached down and punched a button on the dash, locking all the doors.

I yanked on the handle anyway. "I'm getting out."

"No, you're not," he said, still refusing to look at me.

"You can't do this!" I shrieked, the panic warping my voice.

"No one's going to hurt you," Lev said from the backseat. "Relax."

The coarseness of his Russian accent had the opposite effect on my nerves. "Then tell me where we're going."

"My house," he replied.

"Your what?"

His ashen blue eyes searched me. "Just wait and see."

That was the exact opposite of what I intended to do. "No—no. I'm not going. Either you pull over and let me out now, or I'll—"

Or you'll what? You don't even have a phone! Jesus Jesus Jesus...

"Don't be stupid," Lev said, as if reading my thoughts. He reached up and pushed on a panel in the roof of the vehicle. It dropped down to reveal two assault rifles. The weapons were practically bigger than he was. Lev tossed one on the seat and slung the other over his shoulder.

I didn't know if he meant that as a threat or not, but I certainly took it as one.

I turned back around and scanned the road, searching for a landmark. Nothing looked familiar. Then Jayde turned a corner, and a quaint clock tower appeared. I'd seen the iconic image in many a stock photo and knew exactly where we were: Brookline.

Thankfully the suburb was only fifteen minutes from Allston. If I could get away from Jayde, I could easily call for help or catch a bus ride back to the Vons.

I watched the street, making note of all the open businesses where I could seek refuge. Coolidge Corner was busy enough—it was a tourist trap, after all—but the further we drove down the road, the thinner the crowds became, and the dirtier the buildings. Coolidge had been propped up with a constant flow of government funding, but the surrounding district had been left to die. The buildings grew rapidly more dilapidated until they were abandoned entirely.

We finally reached a dead end; the road was blocked off by a gate emblazoned with the United seal and a stiff warning against trespassing.

"We're here." Jayde parked the car and reached back to accept the rifle Lev handed to him. My hopes of making a break for it evaporated.

Jayde finally turned and met eyes with me. "Make this easy and I'll get you home in time."

I swallowed and got out of the car.

Ahead, the whole block was cordoned off with electrified chainlink. It probably wouldn't have stopped a determined vandal—and, judging by a few gaps in the fence, it hadn't—but it certainly looked official. It definitely wasn't the kind of place Andromeda should be seen.

"I don't think we—I—should be here," I stammered.

"I've got clearance," Jayde said, but that fact did nothing to ease my anxiety. He walked up to the gate and pressed his thumb against the keypad. It chirped, and the whole fence crackled as the electricity turned off. He shoved the gate open. "Let's go."

Once more the will to refuse flashed through me, but Lev walked up behind me, his hand on the strap of his gun.

Oh God, protect me, I muttered as I followed Jayde through the gate.

The street beyond was eerily dark, even though the sun hadn't set. It took me a minute to realize why: The electricity to the block had been cut off. Silent traffic lights hung like blind eyes from sagging wires, and the streetlamps had grown cold. No light shone from any of the storefronts, making the buildings look like soulless skeletons.

The whole block had the vibrancy of a morgue, and it smelled like one, too. Trash decayed in the streets, greasy water stood stagnant on the road, and the air hung stiff and silent. There were no birds, no dogs, not even a rat. The only movement was the dying sunlight glinting off the broken glass that salted the pavement.

Jayde stopped in the middle of the road. "This is Brookline," he announced, even though I was well aware. "It's the biggest Jewish community in Boston. Or at least it used to be."

Suddenly the abandoned buildings and stale air made sense. Like Christianity, it was illegal to be Jewish, whether by creed or by blood. And Jews, based on the few I'd met, were generally not willing to deny either.

Jayde continued walking, the glass crunching under his boots like dried bones. I reluctantly followed, leaving as much of a gap between us as Lev would allow.

"This is what happens when the United razes a whole neighborhood," Jayde narrated, gesturing at the empty buildings. "Nobody noticed when the first wave of unassimilated disappeared—take a few here, take a few there, and the world moves on. Someone else steps in to fill the gap they left at work or school, and you never even know they're gone."

I knew that was true. That's what happened to us.

Jayde stopped in the intersection and faced west, his eyes on something unseen around the corner. "That didn't work with the Jews. There were too many of them, too close together. And when you rip a whole neighborhood up by the roots, sometimes there's no one to fill the void."

I stared into the window of the shop next to me, my face reflecting off the dark glass. "How long has this place been abandoned?"

"Seven years," Lev answered, voice husky. I turned to him and was startled to find that his eyes were wet.

"They took everybody." He shrugged his gun from his shoulders. "They blocked off the street and banged down every door. No one escaped. It was cruelly... efficient."

"In and out in an hour," Jayde muttered.

Lev brushed past me. He abandoned his gun on a rusty park bench and disappeared around the corner. Jayde watched him, his face stretched in an expression I had never seen him wear before: Regret.

I stayed where I was, glancing between Jayde and the gun. "What happened to them? Did they take them to a containment camp?"

"No," Jayde snapped. The answer was quick—angry.

I looked up. He flicked his hand at me.

I shook my head. "No."

"Yes," he said, and gestured again. "You need to see this."

I backed up.

He shifted his gun. "You're not leaving until you do."

I took one step forward, then another.

"Not everyone is as lucky as you, Phil. Not everyone gets put up in an apartment paid for by the government."

"It was a prison," I reminded him.

He glanced at me. "These people never made it to prison." He pointed straight ahead.

Inertia carried me forward as the blood pounded in my ears, drowning out all other sound. I rounded the corner and saw that Jayde was right.

These people never made it to a containment camp.

The world spun around me and flashed white and black. I stood completely still, my heart frozen and the prayers dried on my tongue.

Oh Lord, have mercy.

Jayde came and stood beside me. "This is where I met him." He gestured at Lev, who knelt at the edge, motionless.

"Is he…?"

Jayde nodded.

My heart broke free and rammed itself against my ribs. "Then his family…"

Jayde nodded again. I pinched my eyes shut and waited for the roar of grief to subside. Lev would have been only seven, maybe eight.

My eyes flew open as my mind reached the horrible conclusion. "But if you were there…"

Jayde bravely met my eyes. "Someone had to pull the trigger."

I slapped my hand over my mouth.

"It was my first big assignment. I thought we were going in to do another relocation, but not that day. I didn't realize what was happening until they gave the order to open fire." He fingered the strap of his rifle. "That's when I realized I'd joined the wrong side of the war."

I tried to decide whether that confession should inspire fear or admiration—maybe neither.

"But Lev…" I ventured.

"He was supposed to die, too. But I missed."

I didn't ask whether the misfire had been accidental or planned. I knew it didn't matter.

"I came back for him later." Jayde looked back up at Lev, and I saw a roulette of emotions in his eyes: guilt, grief, responsibility, love.

All the emotions I didn't know he was capable of.

Jayde let out his breath. "Brookline won't be the last. Things are changing. The government is tired of paying for the room and board of a bunch of noncompliants. There's talk of relocation, of condensing the camps—or worse."

I didn't have to ask what "or worse" meant.

Assimilated or removed.

"If we're going to stop them, we have to do it now. We have to act while people are paying attention—while they're angry. Your videos made them angry. They will shoot if we give them a target. But if we wait—if we let this die—then people will forget about us, about you, about the camps, about the unassimilated. They'll forget, and then the United can do whatever they want. No one will even know we're gone."

He turned to me, and I knew what he was going to say before the words left his mouth.

"We need you, Blue Fire."

"Jayde, I..." I tried to shift through the emotions that washed over me, but all I was left with was a muddy mess. "You know why I can't. Andromeda can't go on air."

"No," he agreed, and the admission silenced the argument I had ready to follow. "But Philadelphia can."

"I don't... I don't understand."

"I don't need Andromeda—I need Philadelphia. You don't have to disguise yourself to go on air. You can just be you."

I instinctively reached up and fingered my blonde braid. *Just be me?* But I was Andromeda—wasn't I? Did Philadelphia even exist anymore?

"But my prints..." I shook my head. It didn't matter how much makeup I had or didn't have; I couldn't put my family at risk like that. "If I get caught, and they find out about my file, it will implicate Nic and the Vons. I can't do that to them—to Nic."

I braced myself for the angry arguments, but they never came. Instead, he studied me, eyes roaming up and down as if I were a code to be cracked.

"There was a time when Nic was willing to fight for freedom," he said finally. "He was willing to risk a world war just to save a few."

He wasn't wrong, and that made me furious. "Yes, but he's different now," I snapped.

Jayde arched one eyebrow. "Is he?"

"Yes!"

"How?"

I scrambled to put the feeling—the feeling I wasn't sure I even understood—into words.

Jayde beat me to it. "It's because he cares about you."

The revelation wasn't a surprise to me, but it still flooded me with emotion to hear it spelled out from a stranger's lips.

The door's still open.

"That's why he was willing to help you find your father, even though he knew it was a death sentence. If not for you, then for him. He knew what was going to happen."

Look, I'm aware Andromeda has put herself—and, quite frankly, the rest of us—in a dangerous position. But that was her choice.

"He's not stupid, Phil. He knew what could happen. You said yourself today—it was a risk he was willing to take."

He was right, and with each word, I felt like he was chipping away the ground I stood on. Nic did care, and he knew the risks— that's why he hadn't wanted me to go in the first place. That's why he told me to keep my head down.

That's why he wanted me to come back to Mars.

I think you know what I would do.

"Do you care about Nic, Phil?"

"Of course," I said, even though I knew I was walking down a path I'd regret.

"Would you risk your life to save him?"

Pretty sure I've already done that a couple of times. I frowned at Jayde and didn't gratify him with a response.

He didn't wait for one. "Then why won't you sacrifice for your friends in the camps?"

All my excuses evaporated as I skipped my next breath.

"They're still your friends, aren't they? Cami, Aid…"

Their faces flashed before my eyes as the near-forgotten names echoed in my ears.

"What about Stanyard's parents? Don't you think he wants to see them again?"

I wasn't so sure about that, but I knew Stanyard's family was worth fighting for—just as mine was worth fighting for, broken and shattered though it was.

"I don't know how long they have. I don't know how long we have before the camps end up like this." Jayde gestured at the shell of a neighborhood around us. "If the United has its way, soon all the unassimilated will be like Lev's family."

I looked to where the teen knelt on the concrete, weeping over the graves of his people.

Would my people be next?

"You can save them, Phil." Jayde drew my attention back to him. "You can fix this. Blue Fire can."

I can fix this.

I looked into his eyes. He dropped his defenses and spread his hands, the vulnerability rushing back into his face. "Please. Help me."

I didn't answer him. I didn't know what the correct answer was, not anymore.

What do I do, God?

"What… what are you asking me to do?" I whispered.

Something close to a smile stretched his lips. "The same thing you've been doing. I need you to get on there and tell people it's time to fight back. Turn over tables of chemicals, light a weapons factory on fire, get on social media and tell the world the truth—whatever they need to do."

He was right—I'd done all of those things. And I'd do them all again if it meant saving one family, one life.

"But how is that supposed to end the concentration camps?" I asked, desperately hoping there wasn't a catch.

He was grinning now. "If we all stand up together, they can't make us all sit down."

He traced in the air like he was drawing on a map. "Operation Blue Fire isn't an assault; it's a demonstration. If we can rally people across the country to all stand up and break something on the same day, they won't be able to catch us all. You can crush scattered resistance, explain away a lone factory fire with clever media coverage. But you can't silence us all. Not if we speak together. If we knock the legs out, the table will collapse."

His plan made sense—terrifying, exhilarating sense.

We can do this.

"I'm not asking you to lead a war, Phil." He silenced my unspoken fear. "I don't need another soldier. I just need you. I need you to get on there and remind them there's something worth fighting for."

What's worth fighting for? I thought I knew the answer to that question. God was worth fighting for. My family was worth fighting for. Innocent lives were worth fighting for.

Was Operation Blue Fire worth fighting for?

You never should have quit.

"Or." Jayde shouldered his gun, letting the word linger. "You can go back to Mars and live your life as Andromeda Nolan. That's what you want, isn't it?"

There was accusation in his eyes and his tone, and I didn't know how to answer him.

Is that what I really want?

He started walking away. "You can do it. I won't stop you. Take your money and your fancy file and run. Let Earth figure out its own problems."

He stopped at the corner. I turned to watch him.

"Maybe Asia was right," he said without looking back. "Maybe you are one of them."

He continued towards the car. I stared after him, my thoughts and prayers clashing like waves in a hurricane.

You don't belong here, Andromeda.

"For such a time as this."

I started. Lev appeared beside me, his elbow almost brushing mine. His eyes were dry and his face had been rearranged into the stoic expression I was used to from him.

"What?" I asked.

He didn't repeat himself. He just pressed something into my palm.

It was a star of David pin, its silver crusted with dirt and ash.

I looked up into his face. He saluted.

I stared into his white-washed eyes for a long moment. Then I closed my fist around the pin.

20

"Captain on the bridge."

Everyone in the command center shifted to welcome me. I forced myself to return the salutes with nods, even though I felt frail and drab next to all of them. They were all so practiced and precise, with their pressed uniforms and shiny guns. I looked out of place in jeans and Stanyard's hoodie, the most non-descript outfit I could find, my hair pinned up under a scarf. I'd removed my piercings and my contacts. I didn't even have any makeup on.

I stumbled as my feet questioned my decision. *Can I really do this?*

Jayde steadied me. "Relax. Just be yourself."

I nodded, a frantic motion that looked more like a seizure, and followed him across the room.

Tower and Ephesus were there, adjusting the settings on the camera. It was nothing like the setup Thames had rigged. On Mars, I had a whole soundproofed studio to myself. Here, they'd wired a camera directly into the command module. I would be in the center of the action, the entire database at my fingertips, just like the other officers.

Because, in a way, I was one.

Ephesus came to stand beside me. He gripped my elbow and bent over until his lips nearly brushed my ear. "Is this what you want?"

It didn't matter what I wanted anymore. I knew that now.

"It's what Dad should have done," I said, glancing at Tower.

He nodded.

"Then I'm with you." Ephesus squeezed my arm and went to stand on the other side of the terminal.

Jayde dropped a pair of earbuds into my hand. "You'll need these."

I put them in, and the noise of the room faded away, replaced by an unfamiliar voice doing a sound check. But I could still hear Jayde when he spoke, his voice dampened but sharp.

"Are you ready?" It was a question, an invitation—my last chance to walk away.

My answer felt disembodied, echoing back to me through the earbuds, but even I could hear the confidence in my voice. "I'm ready."

He guided me over to the terminal and centered me in front of the camera. The playback flickered on, and my face appeared on the curved monitor. The lighting was dank and gloomy, which was just as well. You couldn't tell what color my hair was, let alone where I was streaming from.

Jayde's voice came through the earbuds. "All systems go?"

"All systems go, lieutenant."

Lev joined the conversation. "Just press the button when you're ready, Blue Fire."

I looked up to see him staring at me from across the terminal. He mouthed the words *thank you.*

I swallowed, suddenly too nervous to acknowledge him.

Someone brushed my hand—Stanyard. He stood in the shadows, just out of sight of the camera. He didn't say anything. He just reached his hand below the control panel and wove his fingers with mine.

I searched his face for an answer, permission, admiration, anything. But there was none. His face was blank, eyes calm and steady. He wouldn't tell me what to do.

Because this was my choice.

I looked down at the terminal. The *start stream* button glowed red and inviting.

The line went silent as everyone waited.

I closed my eyes and counted down, just like Thames used to do.

Holy Spirit, teach me what to say.

I gripped Stanyard's hand and pressed the button. There was a subtle beep, and the timer started ticking up.

I looked into the camera. My face on the screen was pale and haunting, cast into sharp relief by the uneven lighting. But my eyes glistened deep and clear as I opened my mouth and spoke with a confidence that was not my own.

"This is Blue Fire. If you're hearing this, I need your help."

TO BE CONTINUED...

CATALYST
RED RAIN #4.5
RACHEL NEWHOUSE

THERE'S MORE TO THE STORY...

"Where have you been? I thought you were dead!"

That was an exaggeration—I'd only been offline for twenty-four hours, not nearly long enough to send out a search party. But the utter anguish in my wife's voice told me that she had, in fact, assumed the worst. Her shriek made the connection crackle as she continued to scream into the phone.

"I don't get a call, text, nothing. I tried to call you twenty times!"

That was *not* an exaggeration. As soon as they'd given me my devices back, I'd turned on my phone and knew I was in trouble. Abigail had tried to call me at least once an hour, and judging by the timestamps on her barrage of texts, she hadn't slept all night.

I ducked into an alcove behind a potted plant, the only place in the hallway not in full view of a security camera. "Baby, I'm so sorry, but I promise it's fine—"

"It is *not* fine! You go offline while you're in Beijing with all those communists—"

"Abigail," I said, raising my voice to make myself heard. "Remember this is a work line. It's recorded."

She let out a breath that turned into a sob. "I know, I know, I'm sorry, I just... what was I supposed to think?"

I didn't blame her. Being an unassimilated in Beijing, the seat of United politics in the East, was about as safe as walking the streets of Roxbury alone at night. By all accounts, I shouldn't be here. But the government's desire to see an important chemistry research project finished had outweighed their need to be legalistic, and I'd gotten special clearance.

"I know, baby, I'm sorry. Some government officials came to oversee the project, and there was a communications blackout."

"And you couldn't warn me?"

I weighed the tone of my voice before speaking. "They didn't give us any heads up before going in."

Abigail muttered something under her breath, but thankfully she seemed to accept that explanation.

I hated lying to my wife, but she was so scared already. I couldn't imagine what she'd do if she found out the truth.

"Smyrna!" Liu, one of my lab partners, rounded the corner. "How was solitary?"

I slapped my hand over the phone and glared at him. Thankfully he'd barked it at me in Mandarin, but it'd be just my luck that Abigail would remember enough from high school and be able to translate.

"What's going on?" Her muffled voice came from the speaker.

"Just a second, honey, I need to give something to a coworker." I muted the call.

"Sorry," Liu muttered. "I just wanted to know if you still had the notes for the project."

I searched his face. "Which ones?"

He cast a glance around the deserted hall. Turning his back to the security camera, he opened his tablet and pulled up a screenshot. It was a crude drawing of a bird with a lightning bolt in its claws: a thunderbird.

I nodded and swiped through menus on my phone. I knew the officials had deleted my download when they searched my devices, but they clearly hadn't found the backup copies I'd stashed in various places all over the company server.

If they had, I would have been in solitary for much longer than a week.

I found one and initiated the file transfer. I held up my phone, and Liu tapped his tablet on the back of it.

"Thank you," he whispered.

I closed out the window and erased the download. "If anyone else needs it, tell them Chen has backups."

Chen was the lead scientist on the project and a top United official. He'd be mortified to learn that I'd hidden a download link for a Bible on his company profile page, but he was also the person least likely to get implicated if anyone ever found it.

As near as I could tell, they didn't suspect me for transmitting—not yet. They'd caught me reading the Bible on my personal device, which, while a violation of my probationary employment, was hardly something they could imprison me for. I had too many letters after my name to be swept away with the other dissidents. Instead, they added another felony to my file, charged me a huge fine, and stuck me in "special custody" for a day—the United equivalent of a slap on the wrist.

I knew they wouldn't be so merciful if they caught me doing it again, but I couldn't pass up the opportunity to spread Operation Blue Fire in China.

Liu thanked me with a wave and hurried off. I unmuted the call and brought the phone back to my ear. "Sorry about that. I'm here now."

She had apparently used the moment of silence to calm her nerves, because when she spoke her voice was steadier. "You're sure there's nothing I need to know about?"

"I promise," I said with the confidence I knew she was craving. "Everything is fine."

I listened to the silence on the other end of the line and tried to gauge her reaction. Abigail knew what I was doing—sort of. She knew I was transmitting through work, and she knew I'd codenamed the operation after her, in honor of the Bibles she'd shared in high school.

But she had no idea how big the operation had become. She had no idea we'd built a massive network of people willing to transfer restricted media. And she had no idea I was transmitting in China, where the officials were a lot more trigger happy when it came to punishing infractions.

For the sake of her sanity, I didn't want her to find out.

She finally relinquished with a sigh. "I'll just feel better when you get home."

"Which will be very soon." I pumped some reassuring cheer into my voice. "The project is almost done." I probably would have completed it already had I not wasted a perfectly good workday in solitary.

"Good." Her voice caught on the word. "Baby, there's something I need to tell you..."

I stiffened. "What is it? What's wrong?"

"Nothing's wrong," she said, too quickly. "It's just…"

I rattled off a prayer to dampen the panic spiking my nerves. "Do you not want to tell me on a recorded line?"

"No, no, nothing like that. It's…" She sucked in a sharp breath and found her courage. "I'm pregnant."

AVAILABLE NOW!

WANT EXCLUSIVE BONUS SCENES?

Become a Patron and get access to **exclusive bonus scenes** for this book! This bonus content is not available anywhere else, and I post a new scene every month. Plus, you can get digital ARCs, signed paperbacks, collector's edition hardbacks, and merch, or read my WIP as I write it!

Become a Patron at:
patreon.com/rachelnewhouse

Or sign up for my newsletter and be the first to hear about new releases—plus get sneak peeks of upcoming books, cover art, and more!

Sign up at:
rachelnewhouse.com/subscribe

DID YOU LOVE THIS BOOK?

Please consider leaving a review on Amazon or
Goodreads! It's one of the most important things you
can do to support an indie author. Thank you!

HI FROM RACHEL

Rachel Newhouse is an author, wife, secretary, and Sunday school teacher from Kansas City, Missouri. Her obsessions are sci-fi, dystopian, and kid lit. When she's not writing, she's cooking Asian food, growing chilis that are too spicy to eat, and watching wildly age-inappropriate shows like *My Little Pony* and *Gravity Falls* with her husband, Joe. She also really likes glitter. You've been warned.

Connect with Rachel:
bio.site/rachelnewhouse

9 781957 432137